The True Princess

Lacy Williams

Chapter One

"I am a princess, and you will do my bidding."

Tirith, princess of Glorvaird, generally expected capitulation. If she gave an order, it was followed.

But she was out of her element. She was standing in the barn on her father's ranch and the horse standing in the open stall only stared at her, unblinking. The animal was so dark brown that it was almost completely black, all except a white blaze down its nose.

The horse was also taller than Tirith.

With hooves that could break her foot if one stepped on her. Teeth that could bite a finger off if she got too close.

If she ever managed to get the thing saddled and climbed on, she could easily fall and break her neck.

This was a disaster waiting to happen.

"This is for Maggie," she told the horse. And herself. Her twin sister was the head of the family's American-based charitable foundation and had organized a series of events over the next few weeks. A chili cook-off, a silent auction, a ball.

Oh, and a rodeo.

Who'd even heard of a charity rodeo?

Apparently, people from Texas.

In Tirith's experience, many Americans obsessed over royalty. Maggie's husband, Luc, had urged her to take advantage of her connections, and Maggie had run with the idea. Luc had been born in Glorvaird and he and Maggie split their time between the palace and the ranch. He was absolutely besotted with Maggie. And he was Tirith's former best friend.

Maggie had convinced their younger sister Beatrix and their mother to take a few weeks out of the summer schedule to fly out and make appearances. Both would compete in the chili cook-off, along with Tirith.

Their cousin, heir to the throne, Valentin, would attend the charity ball, along with his fiancée.

And Maggie was planning to ride barrels—was that even the right term?—in the rodeo. She'd asked Tirith to be a part of the opening ceremonies. She meant for Tirith to ride out into the arena, holding a flag. Probably wearing a glittering cowgirl shirt with her hair teased into a big-as-Texas style.

After what Maggie had done for her, how could Tirith say no?

She couldn't.

Which was why she'd waited until her sister and father vacated the barn. She hadn't been on horseback since she'd been bucked off as a pre-teen and had badly broken her arm. She had to figure out how to do this without making a fool of herself.

"I'm not afraid of you," she said.

But as she tugged on the rope she'd clipped to the horse's halter, the animal shook its massive head and whinnied.

Tirith startled and dropped the rope.

"I'm not sure he believes you."

The male voice from behind sent her whirling. She raised a hand to press against her pounding heart.

She didn't recognize the cowboy standing in the wide barn aisle. He had his arms crossed with one hand pressed to the underside of his opposite forearm. What a strange way to stand. He looked like any of the other ranch hands she'd seen around over the past few days since her arrival. He wore a T-shirt and grungy jeans above his scuffed cowboy boots. He had at least two days of scruff on his chin, making him look disreputable. And his cowboy hat was pulled low, blocking his eyes from her view.

"May I help you?" She said the words with the same amount of ice she reserved for nosy reporters. She didn't want or need an audience right now.

His lips twitched as if he were amused. "I should probably ask you that. You trying to saddle up?"

It couldn't have been more obvious, thanks to the saddle she'd toted from the tack room and slung over the stall wall.

"I do not require assistance," she said stiffly.

He made a skeptical humming noise that crawled right under her skin. But he said, "I could use some. Assistance. Maybe a bandage."

He raised his arms, and she saw blood dripping between his fingers.

For a millisecond, the bright red of his blood sent her spiraling back to a scene she would rather not remember. She had to blink away the memories.

And then, she jumped into action. "Go into the washroom." She pointed to a door next to the tack room.

He bristled, but she went on.

"I'll bring the first aid kit."

His expression cleared. She didn't know what that moment had been about. Did he dislike taking orders from a woman? Or maybe she'd wounded his pride with the basic instruction.

She didn't have time to dwell on it.

Before she could step away, he drawled, "Better

close the stall door, *highness*. You don't want your mighty steed wandering off."

His use of "highness" was more mocking than anything else. Not a term of respect, that was certain.

But he was right, so she quickly latched the stall door, jumping back when the horse arched its neck over.

She hurried down the hall to the small room tucked at the back of the barn. She knew her father and Maggie shared a large, open office in the farmhouse. This barn office was full of odds and ends, paperwork with columns of numbers she didn't understand. But when her father had given her a quick tour two days before, she'd noticed the red-and-white first aid kit tucked on a high shelf.

She was forced to stand on the wobbly desk chair to reach it.

When she approached the washroom, she could see the cowboy's shoulders from behind. He was standing at the sink, running water.

He was so broad he almost filled up the small space.

A prickling of nerves made her steps falter. She straightened her spine and stepped close.

She wasn't used to being in close proximity with strangers. Her life in Glorvaird was very different than the reality of this Texas ranch. Back home, she was shepherded through her day by her personal assistant.

Her diary was full of appointments and meetings, appearances and events. She had her duty to the crown.

But she also had a duty to her family. And her father would want her to help one of his hired hands.

Her father had been a Navy SEAL before he'd married her mother. He was careful. Protective. She knew he would've done comprehensive background checks on anyone he allowed on the ranch.

So she did her best to put aside the nerves tumbling in her stomach.

She edged into the doorway and caught sight of the cowboy's injury in the mirror hanging above the sink. A three-inch gash on the underside of his forearm was still bleeding freely as he attempted to wash it out.

She felt her stomach lurch as the sight of that blood pinged the sensitive memory. This time, she couldn't push it away fast enough, and her face flushed hot and then cold.

The image of a little girl's crumpled body lying in the street flashed over her vision. She couldn't seem to catch her breath.

"Something the matter, highness?"

The cowboy's casual address startled her back into the present.

She met his eyes in the mirror. He'd pushed his hat back on his head, and she was caught by just how blue his eyes were. She couldn't quite read his expression. Mocking?

"You should call me Tirith," she said. "Not highness."

Edward felt a beat of relief as the color returned to the princess's face. The last thing he needed was for her to faint and someone to come investigate.

As an investigative journalist, Edward had been on dangerous assignments before. But there was something deadly about the princess's father, who was former special ops.

Edward had been hired on as a temporary ranch hand for a couple of weeks to help with the charity rodeo and whatever else the boss needed. He'd been on the ranch for all of three days, and he wasn't going to compromise his cover now.

"Shouldn't you see a doctor?" she asked. "That gash looks like it might need stitches."

His gash had been carefully orchestrated to put him in this very position—close enough to speak to the princess.

"If you've got a butterfly bandage in there, I'll be fine." He nodded to the first aid kit.

She reached for the latch and bobbled the case, almost dropping it.

"Here, switch places with me," he said.

She hesitated minutely as he stepped out of the way, then brushed past him to set the first aid kit on the narrow counter.

He stepped back in front of the sink, effectively trapping her in the tiny bathroom.

Words bubbled up inside him.

What about Peyton? My brother? Don't you feel any remorse?

But he couldn't ask those questions. Not yet.

She glanced up briefly as she unlatched the case. Their gazes clashed for a beat, and something stirred uncomfortably in his gut. Probably indigestion from being so close to a lying cow.

He studied her as she rifled through the first aid kit. He'd been trying to get close to her since he'd arrived, but this was the first chance he'd had to talk to her.

He hated her for what she'd done to Peyton, what she'd cost Carrick back in Glorvaird, but that didn't stop him from noticing the fine bone structure of her face and the sweep of lashes against her cheek. Her glossy, dark ponytail had fallen over her shoulder, and he had the strange urge to tug it like he would've back in grade school.

A faint blush was rising in her cheeks, and he realized he was staring.

Surely she had to be used to that. She was in the public eye all the time.

Was he making her uncomfortable? A part of him rejoiced at that, but he had to stay focused. He needed her to learn to trust him, and he didn't have much time.

Making her uncomfortable was for later.

"How did you cut yourself?" she asked.

"Brushed up against a protruding nail. Accidentally." He tacked on the lie with no remorse. *She* was the liar. One or two white lies were well worth it if they would get her to divulge the truth.

In reality, he'd leaned into the nail on purpose. He'd been working with two other guys on building the temporary holding pens, fifty yards past the barn. He'd seen the princess slip inside the barn and needed an excuse to get close to her. He'd pretended the cut was an accident, and the ranch foreman had waved him off to find a bandage. He couldn't drag this conversation out for long, but it was a start.

She held up a large square paper-wrapped bandage. It would do.

"What exactly were you doing with that horse?" he asked. She wasn't dressed for riding, not in the expensive dove-colored slacks and silk blouse. Her leather boots were quality, but not made for the barn. The boardroom, maybe.

She ripped the package open. "That's none of your

concern." Her words brooked no argument. And made him immediately want to argue.

"Whatever you say, highness."

"What's your name?" This time, her words were a demand.

He swallowed back a refusal. Forced his facial muscles to relax. "Edward."

He'd grown up in Glorvaird but he'd been on enough overseas assignments since secondary school that he'd lost most of his accent. The rest he obscured with a bit of Texas twang.

He didn't give his last name. Simpler was easier.

He'd given her father a fake name, a false identity he'd used before on undercover jobs. The name had a driver's license and social and filed taxes. It must've held up to Gideon Hale's background check, because he hadn't been fired.

He had been pleasantly surprised to be accepted so easily by the other cowboys. The bunkhouse was home to four full-time hands, and four other guys had been hired on temporarily. The guys could be ornery and play pranks, but they watched out for each other.

The Triple H Ranch would be a decent place to land, if he were a cowboy and not a reporter.

She ripped the paper off the bandage, and he lifted his arm, pretending that he couldn't easily reach. "D'you mind?"

She was frowning but didn't refuse.

Her fingers circled his wrist. He wasn't one for romance drivel, but at her touch, a physical shock traveled through his nerve endings, startling him into stillness.

He met her gaze, saw the surprise mirrored in her eyes.

She'd felt it too.

She lowered her eyes quickly, her focus on his arm as she pressed the butterfly bandage over his skin. Again, that telltale flush rose in her cheeks.

The attraction was completely unexpected.

He was a little disgusted with himself. She was an awful person. The kind of person who did something horrible and then covered it up.

But maybe he could use a mutual attraction to get close to her.

He checked the bandage. No leaks. It was tight to his skin. "I appreciate your help. But I'm pretty sure your father is going to fire me if I let that horse run you over. Do you want to tell me what you were doing?"

She kept her eyes on the first aid kit as she tucked everything back inside. "I'd like to go for a ride."

There was something else. Something she wasn't saying.

"Your dad is a horseman. And I bet you've got a big stable at your castle back home."

Her head stayed down. "Good guess."

"But... you don't like horses?"

Her lips firmed into a line. "I like them fine."

No, she didn't. The way she'd shied around the gelding was proof.

"You're scared of them."

Her head came up, and he witnessed the return of the ice princess. She glared at him. "I don't remember asking for you to psychoanalyze me."

She picked up the first aid kit, holding it against her middle, and brushed past him.

He followed at a slow walk. "Your sister's horses are pretty gentle."

Margaret Hale ran an equine therapy program, and her horses were so tame they were practically asleep.

The princess muttered something under her breath as she stalked off to what he thought was the barn office.

He waited in the aisle next to the stall where all this had started.

Moments later, she appeared again.

She didn't look happy to see him standing there.

"Don't you have to get back to work?"

He did. He didn't want Miles to come looking for him. No reason to raise suspicions.

"What if you worked up to it?" he asked. "Put the saddle on the horse today. Maybe tomorrow you ride."

She frowned.

"Why is it so important?"

Her chin jutted up. "I told my sister I'd ride in the opening ceremony for her rodeo."

"The rodeo isn't for another couple weeks. You've got time. Build up to it."

She crossed her arms over her chest, and her chin twisted to the side so he had only a view of her profile. "I'll consider it."

It was an obvious dismissal.

And he still needed to get on her good side.

"I'm happy to help. Anytime. I owe you one." He lifted his arm so the bandage was visible.

She was considering it when he glanced over his shoulder at the outside door. She was still staring at the horse with the stall door closed.

He was a little surprised she hadn't weaseled her way out of the commitment. Why hadn't she told Margaret no?

But he wasn't as surprised as he'd been to feel the instant connection when she'd touched him.

There was attraction there—on his part and hers. Now, all he needed was a way to capitalize on it.

Chapter Two

Edward held his palm against the scratch beneath the left side of his jaw. He threw open the door to the bunkhouse.

The princess jumped and whirled from the counter where she had been standing. She looked vaguely guilty, and his glance quickly encompassed the items laid out on the kitchen counter. Ground beef, a whole cabinet full of spices, a couple of cans of beans. Nothing nefarious. So why had she jumped like a startled deer?

"Don't mind me." He headed for the bathroom.

The bunkhouse was one long building. Less like a house and more like an apartment for college guys.

The kitchen ran along all of one wall, with a long counter interrupted by the stove and fridge at one end. A big window looked over the nearest field. A long dining table broke up the open room, and on the other side of it a living area was filled with a scuffed leather couch, a couple of chairs, a coffee table marked with rings, and a TV that was usually tuned to sports or news.

At one time, someone had attempted to decorate in a western style. A horseshoe was hung over the doorway. A beautiful painting of a horse galloping through a meadow hung on one wall.

But what might've once been tasteful had been disrupted by the dartboard hanging next to the painting and several ball caps had been tacked in a pattern on another wall.

The bunkhouse was most definitely the domain of several bachelors.

Past the living area was the bedroom, where half a dozen bunks and three dressers were located. And the bathroom, which was Edward's destination.

This morning was the first time he'd caught a glimpse of the princess since he'd run into her in the barn three days prior.

Miles had kept the regular ranch hands and the extra hired cowboys busy from dawn until dusk.

They'd moved cattle, pushing a big herd from one of the fields closer to the house and barn to a pasture two miles away. They'd finished constructing the holding pens and temporary chutes for the arena.

And then there were the patrols.

Edward had stumbled over that secret accidentally when he had woken coughing in the night, his allergies acting up after being outdoors in the dust. He'd gone to the kitchen to get a glass of water. That big window above the kitchen sink didn't hide a thing, and he'd easily seen two men on horseback who had passed each other in the field.

Each one had a rifle strapped to his saddle.

One walked his horse toward the barn; the other disappeared out of sight toward the fields.

In the dark, he hadn't been able to identify the men. But he recognized a security patrol when he saw one.

What he didn't know was why it was needed.

There was already a visible security team guarding the house. Unobtrusive cameras around the ranch and the gated entrance. Why did they need riders on horseback?

His gut told him there was a story here. His editor had given him the go-ahead to chase it.

He stared at his reflection in the water-spotted mirror. His fingers were still clamped over the new scratch he'd given himself, this one behind his jaw and under his ear.

He'd tanned, being out in the sun all day. The color in his face highlighted the tiny lines around his eyes. He'd hit his mid-thirties, and his body refused to do the tasks he'd done easily when he was twenty. He was exhausted from the strenuous work.

He was chafing with inactivity on the princess front. He wanted justice for Peyton, for Carrick. He'd like to return to Glorvaird and check on his niece in person.

He hadn't told his brother he was coming to the U.S. or about his self-imposed mission. He wasn't supposed to know that the princess had been negligent and caused a car accident. His niece had broken multiple bones, but the biggest injury was the TBI— traumatic brain injury. Almost six weeks ago now, he'd gone to visit his family only to find them out of the house late at night. His curiosity had been piqued, and when he'd seen Carrick's email open on his computer in his home office... he'd snooped.

And discovered the truth, including a scanned copy of the non-disclosure agreement his brother had signed.

It had stung, knowing Carrick had kept the truth from him, though he understood why Carrick had been forced to.

The crown didn't want its sterling reputation tarnished.

Edward blamed the princess for all of it, but whatever remuneration Carrick was receiving—that had to be the reason he'd signed the NDA—was on the line.

No one could know that Edward had found out the truth behind the accident.

If he was going to out the royal family, he had to dig up the dirt on his own. It had taken months to set this up.

And to achieve his aim, he needed to be close to the princess.

His impatience had come to a head this morning, and he'd been lucky to see her sneaking out to the bunkhouse.

He'd manufactured another injury, and the cowboy who'd been helping him load up a farm truck with barbed wire and metal fence poles had waved him off to clean it up in the bunkhouse.

After today, he wouldn't be able to use an injury again.

There was accident-prone and there was suspicious, and he was already walking a fine line.

He turned on the faucet and pulled his fingers away from the wound, wincing as blood dripped down his neck. He hadn't meant to make the cut quite so deep.

It didn't matter. Even if he ended up scarred, getting justice for Peyton would be worth it.

He pressed some tissue from the bathroom against his new wound and found a first aid kit in the cabinet beneath the sink. He set it on the counter and then moved to stand in the doorway, facing the princess.

She stared out the kitchen window with her arms crossed, her hands holding onto her elbows. She looked a little lost. She glanced over her shoulder and caught sight of him.

"Will it offend your delicate sensibilities if I ask for your help again?" he asked.

She seemed to blink away whatever thoughts were plaguing her. "What does that mean? My 'delicate sensibilities'?"

He shrugged. "I guess it doesn't seem like you belong here. Branding steers and pulling calves." *Riding horses.*

She wore a fancy blouse again, though today she wore slim-fitting dark jeans and sneakers.

She started across the room toward him. "Do you belong here?"

"Miles is a good boss. I like working outdoors."

She brushed past him into the bathroom, and he saw her stiffen when she registered the mess. There were towels on the floor, and had she seen the whiskers on the insides of the sink? Cowboys weren't much for cleaning up after themselves.

She steeled herself, and he handed her the band-aid he'd plucked from the first aid kit. "I don't need a doctor or stitches. I just can't see at a good angle in the mirror."

She moved close and tilted her head to see his scratch. He moved the tissue away and watched her expression in the mirror. She looked serene, almost blank. He'd seen a similar expression on other faces. Celebrities. Actors. Politicians. It was an expression they wore to hide their true feelings.

She had to step closer to reach him as she dabbed at his neck with ointment. She was in his personal space now, and her scent enveloped him. It was lighter than perfume. Maybe her shampoo, or her soap. Jasmine.

She breathed in deeply, and it made him self-conscious of the fact that he'd been out in the barn before sunup. His work hauling supplies that morning had been grueling.

He shifted his feet so that he gained a half-inch of distance. "Don't breathe in too deeply. I'm a sweaty mess."

She turned away to exchange the ointment for his band-aid. In the mirror, he had a view of her profile. There was no mistaking the flush that started in her throat and rose into her cheeks.

"There." She pressed the bandage against his skin, and he felt another *zing* of attraction.

After which, she rushed out of the bathroom.

He put away the first aid kit then strode through the living area to find her at the sink, washing her hands.

He stopped near the dining table. "Was there something you needed?"

She glanced at him over her shoulder as she dried her hands, a question in her expression.

"Somehow I doubt you're in here to make the beds or bring fresh towels." He infused his voice with wry humor.

One corner of her mouth turned up. "I needed a place to cook."

He raised his brows. "Isn't there a kitchen in that big farmhouse?" No doubt it was miles better than the fifteen-year-old appliances and Formica counters in here.

She moved restlessly to where she'd laid out her ingredients.

"You cookin' up a secret?" he asked quietly.

She shook her head, not looking at him. "It's not a secret. But I'd rather my family not watch over my shoulder."

There was something in the way she said the words. Some hurt. Something about her family. His journalistic instincts were buzzing.

"I'm a confirmed bachelor. You want some help? I owe you, after all." He gestured to the bandage when she glanced over at him.

"You cook?"

"Sure." That was an exaggeration. He could make scrambled eggs. And Peyton's favorite: grilled cheese.

He worked a lot. Had never had time to learn to make himself meals. But if it meant getting close to the princess, he could be a chef. "I can follow a recipe," he added easily as he rounded the dining table.

"Won't Miles be expecting you?"

He shrugged. "I can spare fifteen minutes. I'll work overtime later tonight if I need to."

She seemed to accept that. She nudged a piece of paper across the counter to him. A computer-printed recipe. *Texas chili.*

He glanced curiously at her. "I heard about the chili cook off. Don't tell me you're entering."

She fiddled with the spices, lining them up like toy soldiers. "My whole family is participating." There it was again, that uncertainty in her voice. "I don't want to make a fool of myself."

That was exactly the kind of sentiment he'd expected from her. She wanted to save face. Uphold her public image.

"You could always drop out." He had to work to keep the hardness out of his voice.

She shook her head. "My sister's foundation does a lot of good. I want to help." She blinked rapidly and turned her face to the window. She cared that much?

Or she was a good actress.

Except he was the only one here. And she probably didn't care what he thought about her.

So what?

He had written enough exposés to know that everybody was made up of shades of gray. Even the most notorious criminals usually cared about and wanted to take care of their families.

It didn't matter that the princess had a single kind-hearted bone in her body.

She'd been careless and covered it up while his family suffered.

But the knowledge that she wasn't all bad made his stomach twist in a knot.

* * *

Tirith watched Edward hesitate. He'd clearly been on his way to the door, but now he hovered just between the kitchen and the dining table.

There was a part of her that wanted to urge him on.

The man had nearly caught her sniffing him. She'd been standing close to put that silly band-aid on his neck, and she'd been tantalized by the scent of his skin, a mix of Texas grass, saddle leather, and something that was uniquely Edward.

Thank goodness he'd said something about being sweaty and edged away. He'd saved her further embarrassment. She could only pray he hadn't noticed.

It had obviously been far too long since she'd dated. She had her reasons. Edward was the first man in a very long time she'd been attracted to.

"I'm happy to help you get started," he offered

now. "And you've got a crew full of cowboys that'll stampede in here at lunchtime, scrounging for food. They can test it for you. Give you an honest opinion."

She wanted to refuse. Save herself further humiliation. She knew he had to feel the attraction between them too. It had crackled through the air both times they'd been in the same room together.

What was his motive? Had he made the offer out of the goodness of his heart?

She didn't know.

But she was desperate.

And there was a part of her that wanted to stay as far away from the ranch house as possible.

Her mother had arrived that morning, with Bea in tow and an entourage of guards. She'd been cool and distant when she'd greeted Tirith.

It wasn't a complete surprise. Mother had treated Tirith differently ever since Tirith had proposed a new royal initiative. Tirith had battled anxiety for years and wanted to help erase the stigma of mental illness.

Mother had some old-fashioned ideas.

Lately, whatever warmth Tirith remembered from her childhood was gone. Mother hadn't smiled at her in weeks. Not a real smile, anyway.

So Tirith had escaped the ranch house with the excuse of cooking up a practice round of chili. She'd dithered too long in the bunkhouse, long enough for the cowboy to come in and find her staring into space.

She wasn't used to asking for help. In the palace, there was always someone to see to her needs. Sometimes even before she realized what she needed.

Now she smiled a trembling smile at him. "I suppose you could help me get started."

He saw through her attempt at making it seem as if she was the one doing him a favor. Something sparked in his eyes, but he didn't comment.

She was completely inept in the kitchen, and she caught the smile he tried to hide when she didn't know how to use the crank can opener he found in one of the kitchen drawers.

He might be a cook, but he certainly wasn't familiar with this kitchen. While she browned the meat, he opened and closed all six of the drawers, familiarizing himself with their contents.

She knew her father and Maggie hired a cook part time to help feed the ranch hands so that Scarlett didn't have to do all of it. The hired cook, Daisy, used the ranch kitchen. Which meant this kitchen was furnished with only the bare minimum.

Edward muttered about the lack of appropriate utensils, his shoulder brushing hers as he moved around her to fish in one of the drawers again.

He moved with an easy grace that she envied. It had taken her years to learn to relax in her own skin, and she only managed it when she was alone. It was safer that way.

"You're smoking," he cautioned.

She jumped, blinking out of her wandering thoughts. The ground beef in the pan was starting to smoke. What should she do?

"You need to stir." Standing at her back, he reached around her and grabbed the floppy rubber spatula from the counter.

He was too close. Her heart beat in her ears. But he had her boxed in as he stirred the meat in the pan. It stopped smoking and went back to sizzling.

He stepped away and turned on the faucet.

"What's it like, living in Glorvaird?" His question was asked casually. He wasn't looking at her as he rinsed out the can of tomato sauce they'd added to a large pot on the second burner.

But she was still flushed from his close proximity.

And aware that every word she said could end up in a tabloid.

She stuck to her usual public answer. "The countryside at home is like nothing you've ever seen. The seaside cliffs and how the city rises above the water. But what I love most about home are the mountains."

She didn't usually add that last part.

She hadn't thought so as a child. The mountains were inland, remote, too far from the city with its bustling tourism. They were too isolated. It felt as if she could get lost and never be found.

But after the accident, during her recovery, she'd gone away and found herself in the mountains.

"It must be nice, not having to cook for yourself. Always having someone there to look after you."

His words hummed with disgust that he couldn't quite mask.

She heard that tone from people who didn't know her. People who didn't understand that the royal family worked hard for their country. Before the accident, there had been days when she'd been so busy she'd barely had time to eat.

It stung to hear Edward's censure. The fact that it stung was ridiculous.

They didn't know each other.

It was only the connection that flared to life when they were together that made it feel as if they did.

"Ground beef is browned," he said. "You want to add it to the chili pot?"

The skillet was unwieldy, and some of the meat dropped onto the stovetop as she attempted to pour it into the stock pot.

Edward went for the paper towel roll by the sink. "Did you ask your dad to help you ride that horse?"

She shook her head. Her father was an expert horseman. She wasn't ready to admit to him that she hadn't been on horseback in over a decade. "It's impolite to remind a lady about her imperfections."

He snorted slightly. And then, his voice overly

casual, he said, "Your dad's probably been too busy to help, anyway. What with the extra patrols he's got running at night."

She looked up from stirring the pot. "What patrols?"

The morning sun streamed in the window, highlighting the dark stubble at his jaw. "Not sure I'm supposed to know about them—me bein' the new guy and all. But a couple of nights ago, I saw the changing of the guard."

What was he talking about?

He must've recognized her cluelessness. "One guy rode toward the barn. One rode out into the night. Both of 'em had rifles tied to their saddles."

She picked up the skillet and moved to the sink, forcing him to step aside. She ran water into the pan, considering what to say.

Edward spoke before she did. "I might only be a temporary worker, but I'd like to know I'm not going to get shot while I'm riding fences."

A shiver went through her at the thought. "You aren't."

The raise of his brows showed his skepticism.

There were always threats against the crown. Most were anonymous emails or letters. They were all investigated. Most turned out to be nothing.

Occasionally, there was a threat that the royal security team took seriously. Her father had mentioned that there would be heightened security over the next weeks, but she'd thought it was because of Valentin's presence.

But her cousin wasn't set to arrive until just before the ball.

Why would Father have extra patrols now?

"Are you in danger?" His pointed question brought her out of her thoughts. It was past the bounds of curiosity and bordering on nosy.

And she didn't have an answer for him.

"If you have concerns, I'm sure my father or Miles can answer them. You should bring your questions up with them."

His expression closed off. "I might do that."

A soft pop and hiss sounded. He turned to the stock pot and used a long-handled spoon to give it a stir. "This looks decent. We didn't botch it too badly. You want to taste it?"

"I thought it had to simmer for three hours?"

He dipped the spoon into the pot. "You got that right. Cooking it for that long will enhance the flavors, infuse them into the meat. But you can still give it a test and get an idea of what the final product will taste like."

She wasn't expecting him to step toward her and extend the spoon. It felt a little too intimate, but after he had helped her, how could she refuse?

She opened her mouth. Behind the spoon, his gaze

was warm. Almost as smoky as the chili smelled. He gently tipped a small bite into her mouth.

Flavor exploded over her tongue, but not in a good way.

Hot!

She swallowed after barely chewing and lunged for the faucet, quickly turning it on and cupping her hand beneath the stream of water. She drank directly from her hands, mouth burning too badly to be embarrassed.

"Too spicy?"

She couldn't answer him. Her eyes were tearing, and she blinked rapidly, watching as he reached for the drawer and pulled out another spoon. He took a bite for himself. Smacked his lips.

"It's got a kick, all right."

She was still gulping water when he chuckled. "Let me get you some milk. It'll soothe the burn better than water."

She let the rest of the water run off her hands and reached for the towel to dry off as he filled a glass.

She took the milk from him and gulped it down.

"Slow down," he said. He wasn't laughing out loud, but she saw the way his eyes were dancing. "You sure you measured the spices right?"

She nodded. She tried wiggling her tongue inside her mouth. Maybe she hadn't burned every square inch of her taste buds.

"I bet the other cowboys will like it."

She finally got her mouth working. "We can't serve that." So her words sounded more like a gasp than anything else.

"It's Texas chili. Texans don't mind the heat."

She considered dumping the whole thing in the garbage. But she hated to waste it. "Do you really think they'd eat it?"

He smiled. A real smile that made her belly flip. "I'll report back when they come in for lunch."

She wrinkled her nose skeptically, but he didn't seem to see it as he dug a ballpoint pen out of the junk drawer at the end of the counter. He took her hand in his and wrote something on her palm.

His number.

"Text me, and I'll have your number. Then I can let you know about the chili. And you can call me when you're ready to go for that ride."

Her stomach did a second slow flip.

He was flirting with her. Like she was a normal woman, not a princess.

It wasn't real.

But she carried the warm feeling with her all day.

Chapter Three

Tirith would not cry.

She simply refused.

At least not until later tonight, in the privacy of her room.

Although even that wasn't private anymore, not while she and Bea were sharing the small space.

Today was chili cook-off day.

And Tirith didn't have a partner.

The mayor of nearby Taylor Hills was a family friend, and Maggie had cajoled him into taking part in the event. But he'd notified them only an hour before that he had a stomach bug and wouldn't make it.

Tirith didn't look at the spectators milling around the perimeter of the spacious room. The 4-H building was more like an empty warehouse, with a concrete floor and cinder block walls. But it suited Maggie's purposes, and everyone in the community knew where it was.

Bleachers that looked like they belonged in a high school gym had been set up at one end of the room. They were mostly empty, as it was early yet. Maggie's team had cordoned off the center of the area, and a security team was spread throughout, attempting to blend in to the crowd. Some of her dad's cowboys were milling around too. She'd had a brief glimpse of Edward earlier.

While the chili was cooking, Maggie and her dad would hold a short press conference and answer questions about the foundation. When the chili was ready, the crowd would have a chance to taste all of the selections.

There were twelve cooking stations set up around the inside of the roped-off area. Each one had a small countertop with two hot plates that would serve as burners. A cutting board, knives, and assorted utensils made up the rest of the gear each pair of amateur chefs would be allowed to use. There was a central area where all the ingredients were kept. The teams wouldn't be allowed to choose ingredients until the cook-off started.

How was she supposed to do this on her own?

Tirith glanced down at the two pieces of paper on her station—an ingredients list and a rough recipe. She was aware of her father and Bea at the station to her left. Her mother and Maggie were on their other side. Maggie had set it up so the royal family was competing against family friends and prominent local celebrities —like the veterinarian who, based on the way he'd greeted every person by name, knew *everyone* in town, and the high school principal, who'd been surrounded by people since he'd walked in.

A cameraman ducked beneath the barrier, and Tirith chose to squat behind her counter, pretending to search for something on the shelf below. Not her smartest move, since there were only three steel mixing bowls and a cutting board down here.

Maggie had hired a group of kids from the local community college to video today's event and run live segments on the Foundation's social media pages throughout the day. There were four or five of them running around, and since they were approved by Maggie and the security team, Tirith wouldn't be able to avoid them forever.

She usually didn't mind cameras. But today she felt unsettled.

That morning, Maggie had found her sipping a cup of tea in the kitchen. She'd come to break the news that Tirith no longer had a partner for the event.

Mother had been on her heels.

Tirith hadn't blinked when Maggie had asked whether she was good to complete the event on her own.

But Mother's words had been a cut. *"Perhaps you should stay behind the scenes, dear."*

And Tirith had heard what she didn't say aloud. That Tirith couldn't be trusted. Mother looked at her differently now. She thought Tirith might make a scene and ruin Maggie's event.

Mother couldn't have known that her lack of faith in her daughter was sending Tirith perilously close to a panic attack that very moment.

Breathe.

She counted out several slow breaths, her head still bowed, crouched behind her work counter. She focused on listening to what was happening around her. Father was nearby, his voice a calm counterpoint to Bea's bubbly excitement. They were arguing about peppers.

There was a young child somewhere in the crowd, chattering about ice cream flavors. Someone was humming. Outside, the breeze was blowing. It was a sound that belonged to her childhood, the constant Texas wind. Like a little girl, she was still holding onto a childish hope that her mother and father would reconcile someday.

Her stomach felt jittery, but she forced her wobbly legs to hold her as she straightened.

Maggie had posted a large digital countdown timer on one wall. There were five minutes before the official start to the cook-off.

If she was going to do this by herself, she needed a game plan. At least she wasn't flying blind. Edward had helped her practice in the bunkhouse only a few days before, so she knew there were several steps to the process that needed to happen simultaneously. She would just have to juggle.

It was as if thinking about him had conjured his presence.

Edward was at the edge of the roped-off crowd, speaking to one of the security guards.

And then he ducked underneath the barrier and strode toward her.

"Where's your partner?" He stopped on the opposite side of her counter.

"Sick. I'm on my own." She sounded airy and unaffected. But to her horror, her lips trembled.

And he saw.

For a moment, the connection between them—or attraction or whatever it was, a feeling she hadn't been able to name—leapt to life.

He rounded the counter. "You got an extra apron? I won't hold it against you that you never texted me to find out how the hands liked your chili."

It took her a beat too long to realize he meant *he* was going to cook with her.

"You can't just…"

But he was *just*. He'd already removed the blue apron that matched the one she already wore from the hook on the side of the counter and was slipping it over his head.

"I'm employed by the Triple H. That's gotta count for something."

He waved at someone behind her, and she turned her head to see her father watching them. Bea said something to him, and he returned his focus to their workspace.

"Same recipe as before?" Edward's question brought her attention back to her new partner.

"Absolutely not. I still can't taste anything on the right side of my mouth."

He grinned, and her stomach took a tumble. "It turned out all right. The cowboys emptied the pot."

She didn't know why he'd chosen to come to her rescue, to be her partner, but there were thirty seconds left on that countdown clock and she wasn't going to send him away now.

"The old timers in the crowd would give you their vote for that fire alarm chili."

"I would prefer not to involve the fire department," she said primly.

He laughed, a low sound that made her heart pitter-patter. He almost looked... surprised.

Was it so shocking that she could make him laugh?

He glanced away.

Five seconds left.

She picked up the ingredients list from the counter

and quickly ripped it in half. She offered him one of the pieces. "We'll have two minutes to grab all of the ingredients."

His fingers closed over hers briefly as he took the list. "You want me to misplace ingredients while I'm at it? Make it difficult for the other teams?"

She hadn't thought to be that devious. "This is a charity event. We'd better play it safe. No cheating."

"I thought you'd say that."

But when he smiled at her, it didn't feel safe at all.

*　*　*

The royal security force was out *en masse* today. There was definitely something going on.

Which is why Edward had done the stupid thing and joined up with Tirith for the cook-off.

He wanted to find out what all the security was about.

It didn't have anything to do with the pinch in his gut when he'd noticed her hiding behind her counter. Or that her hands had been shaking when she'd swept a stray strand of hair from her face.

He didn't feel sorry for her.

She didn't deserve compassion.

He'd seen a chance and taken it. He wanted the story.

And if this unwanted attraction they shared would get him closer to her, he needed to use it.

They worked together to do the quickest "grocery shop" in history.

"You want to chop?" he asked back at their station.

"Yes. And you'll brown the beef?"

They set to work. He had the ground beef sizzling in a skillet while she chopped a green bell pepper.

He moved to sort through the dry spices she'd tossed in a brown sack. "Lot of security here today. Because of your mom?" He held his breath, waiting for her answer. Had that been too obvious?

Over her shoulder, he caught Gideon Hale shooting him a look from the next station over. It'd been a risk, approaching Tirith in such a public setting. Edward was putting himself under the rancher's scrutiny. He needed his identity to hold up for a little while longer.

Tirith was opening her mouth to answer when a college-aged kid approached, holding some kind of apparatus with a high-tech video camera on top. A second kid was with him and asked Tirith a question about her sister's charity.

Tirith gave an answer that seemed authentic, a smile that was genuine, as she spoke about the children Maggie's foundation was helping and why the work was so important. She was charming and perfectly at ease.

It couldn't be real, could it?

But the kid behind the camera was eating it up. He looked a little star-struck. Or maybe just enthralled by the princess and her beauty.

When Tirith turned that smile on Edward, part of him started to get lost in her magnetism too.

Except he knew better.

He pressed his lips together in an expression that meant to show her he saw through her.

She switched to chopping a jalapeño while the kid asked Edward what he was doing behind the stove.

"I'm usually riding fence lines for the Triple H, but today I found out the princess needed an extra hand, so I volunteered."

The kid didn't seem interested since Edward wasn't anyone famous, and that was fine with him. The less attention shined on him, the better.

Tirith used the cutting board to tip her peppers to the sizzling meat in the skillet. She wiped her hands on her apron.

He was glancing at her from the corner of his eye when he saw her swipe that same strand of hair out of her eyes.

She gasped. Had she seen something? Where exactly was the danger?

But when he looked at her, her eyes were tearing, and the tip of her nose was red.

"What's—?" And then it hit him. "You had oil from that jalapeño on your fingers."

His hand was at her elbow before he'd given it a thought. There had to be a medic here—

She was tugging against his hold. "We can't leave the station. The meat will burn."

She couldn't be worried about the stupid chili at this point. Her eyes were streaming tears. She waved her free hand as if she wanted to touch her face but knew better.

"I barely touched my face." There was a hint of whimper in her voice. "How can it hurt so much?"

"You need to flush your eyes with water."

He looked around. There was an arrow pointing to the restrooms at the back of the building, away from the crowd.

His gazed clashed with Gideon's. Concern was etched on the man's face.

He refocused on Tirith when she spoke. "You stay here and watch the chili."

By now her eyes were completely closed, still tearing.

And then he caught sight of the kid approaching again, camera pointed toward Tirith. He'd somehow caught wind that something was going on.

Edward scowled at him. "Turn the camera off. You can come back to us later." He didn't realize he'd pulled her to his chest until he was looking down into her face. He didn't wait for the kid to follow his instructions but moved the half-done ground beef off of the burner, setting it on the cutting board, where he hoped it wouldn't melt through to the counter below.

"Just point me toward the women's restroom." Was she still arguing with him?

"C'mon." He kept her elbow in his hand and ushered her toward the back of the building. "I took the food off the burner. We'll come right back." Unless she was in bad shape, in which case, someone could drive her to the nearest hospital.

She let him lead her away, one hand shielding her eyes. "I can't believe I made such an amateur mistake." She sighed. "Everyone saw, didn't they?"

"Dunno." He'd been more concerned with her than everyone else.

No one answered his knock on the women's bath-room door, and he pushed inside. He used the lever above the door to prop it open and then led her inside.

"Soap and wash your hands first," he said. "Or you'll spread the oil."

Except, how was she supposed to see the soap dispenser? He turned on the faucet first, then pumped several squirts of soap into his own hands.

It felt entirely too intimate as he lathered her hands over the sink. His fingers moved between hers, smoothed over her palms.

Her eyes were still closed, her face tilted toward him.

As if she trusted him.

His gut clenched into an uncomfortable boulder. He forced himself to guide her hands under the stream of water and let her go. "Okay?"

She made an indecipherable murmur and bent to splash her face.

At the last second, he saved her long ponytail from falling into the sink.

There was no sign of the composed princess as she sought only relief. She even let some of the water run into her mouth.

He grabbed some paper towels and waited.

"Just give me a second," she gasped. "I think I'm all right."

"Good. I think your father might come after me if we're gone too long."

She made a sound that might be a laugh. Grabbed the edge of the sink and straightened. He pressed the paper towels into her hand.

"He's a little overprotective." She blinked and opened her eyes for the first time since they'd left their cooking station. They were red-rimmed. Her makeup had been washed off.

There was something different about the small smile she gave him. Something warm and open.

And it made that rock in his gut burn hotter.

Which was why he said, "Overprotective enough to hire all those extra bodyguards?"

She hadn't answered him back at the station because they'd been interrupted.

Now, his question seemed to put her defenses back up.

Good. That was what he needed. He couldn't think, couldn't remember the real reason he was here, when she looked at him as she had before, with tenderness and trust.

A man in a dark suit appeared in the doorway. Tirith must've seen him in the mirror.

"We're coming," she murmured. Then to Edward, "We've got to get the chili in the pot."

She didn't want to talk about the security. Which only made his curiosity burn hotter.

She leaned closer to the mirror and wrinkled her nose at her bedraggled appearance. He half expected her to call for a makeup person or even refuse to go back out there without a full face of makeup on. But she only straightened her shoulders and made for the door.

He followed, determined to press her about the bodyguards. He was a half-step behind her at the doorway, but as he crossed the threshold, there was a loud explosion. The sound echoed off the high metal ceiling. It had come from inside the building?

He reacted with pure instinct, honed from months of overseas assignments in a war zone.

He grabbed Tirith's waist and pulled her back into the bathroom, around the doorframe so she was behind the cinder block wall. He pressed close, put himself between her and the danger.

What was it? An IED? A grenade?

There was shouting, and he peered around the doorframe to see the security guys in dark suits mobilizing through the crowd. The guy who'd come after them in the bathroom was doubling back.

Edward looked down into Tirith's face. Her eyes were wide and frightened. Her breaths were shallow.

He wanted to comfort her.

He wanted to *kiss* her.

The outlandish thought was replaced quickly as the guard approached. He was listening to some message coming through his earpiece, his weapon out and pointed at the ground.

"We're clear," he said to them—no, to Tirith. "One of the cooks blew the lid off of a pot."

A cooking disaster. That was all it was.

But the princess was shaking. Or maybe he was. She took a moment to smooth out her apron before nodding to the guard, who escorted them back to their station.

If the explosion was nothing, why did Gideon Hale have Princess Alessandra away from her station?

They were talking in low voices—arguing?—behind a wall of three guards.

Others were sweeping through the crowd.

Finally, Tirith's mother and father returned to their stations, though the rancher's expression was like granite.

Tirith noticed Edward noticing all of this. And maybe something had changed between them when he'd pushed her behind him in the bathroom. She leaned in and whispered, "There's been a threat against my mother. An email, I think. She doesn't think it is anything to worry over."

But obviously Gideon Hale didn't agree. The man's gaze flicked through the crowd, not stopping anywhere for long.

"He almost lost her once," Tirith said, voice low. "When they first met." There was nostalgia in her tone, and behind it, sorrow.

That wasn't the information Edward needed, even if it was juicy.

But the camera soon returned to their station, and Edward didn't have a chance to push for more. Not yet.

Chapter Four

Two days after the chili cookoff, a slender figure detached itself from the growing shadows outside the barn as Edward approached on foot.

Tirith.

The sun was setting behind the structure, and he had to squint before he could make her out. Definitely her, and he couldn't explain the beat of relief that coursed through him.

He didn't have to seek her out. Mission on.

That was all it was.

That and the fact that he was exhausted.

He'd been assigned a job repairing fence lines in the far pasture today. He'd suspected he'd been sent so far from the house and barn because Gideon Hale had seen him in close proximity to the princess during the chili cook-off.

Call it a hunch.

His horse had come up lame late in the day. When he'd called in on his two-way radio, he'd been told there wasn't a truck or trailer to send after him. He'd been forced to walk with his horse, and during the long walk under the hot evening sun, he'd wondered how Hale had engineered this punishment.

If he'd known he'd come face to face with the princess at the close of this unending day, it might've made everything worth it.

She had a slightly-too-big cowboy hat smashed low on her head and wore a T-shirt and jeans and boots that might belong to Margaret, because they were faded and broken-in.

He'd never seen Tirith so casual.

The yard was quiet. There were lights on in the farmhouse and bunkhouse, but everyone seemed to be inside. The setting sun was changing the light around them, lengthening the shadows.

"I need to ask you a favor," she asked at his approach. Her head was tilted so that silly hat hid her eyes from him.

He still had the reins in hand. He was exhausted and dirty and desperate for a shower and his bunk.

But this was Tirith. Waiting for him.

He stopped within reaching distance of her, the horse behind him. "What do you need?"

He heard the soft catch in her breath before she cleared her throat. "I was wondering if you'd saddle one of Maggie's horses for me. I'd like to take a quick turn around the corral."

She would, huh?

He let her request hang in the air between them for a long moment. She still hadn't looked up.

"It's almost dark," he said.

They both knew there was a big spotlight for the corral near the barn. It wasn't currently on, but that was an easy fix.

"Why not ask your dad?" he said when she remained quiet.

She shrugged.

What was going on?

He reached out and used his finger to tip her hat up. Her eyes flicked to him, and with her face fully revealed, he saw that she was close to tears. Her eyes were glassy and the tip of her nose was pink.

She was upset.

And she didn't want her dad. She'd come looking for Edward.

That had to mean he was getting closer to what he'd come here for. His gut knotted.

"I've got to take care of this guy first. Then I'll take care of you."

He saw emotion pass over her expression. Usually, she was better at hiding it. Was that gratitude? Or something else?

She trailed him and the horse into the barn, keeping her distance from the animal. He unsaddled the horse and gave it a rubdown and some grain. He'd already told Miles about the lameness. He'd remind the foreman in the morning, make sure the horse got checked over.

He detoured to the tack room and pulled the saddle for the horse the princess had wanted saddled a week ago. He carried it on his shoulder and joined her.

Tirith had hung her hat over one of the posts. When she caught sight of him, her gaze flicked to where his shoulder muscles stretched to carry the saddle.

Either she was getting worse at hiding her emotions from him, or she was letting him in.

He slung the saddle over the stall railing and moved to open the gate. When he reached up for the horse's halter, he did a surreptitious sniff of his armpit. He'd been doing heavy work out in the hot sun. He wasn't fresh, and he wished for a moment that he'd had a chance to shower in the bunkhouse.

Not that that was necessary. Just because she'd sought him out didn't mean she wanted him close.

She'd asked him to saddle the horse for her. *She*

was the one who would be riding around the corral. He'd watch and make sure she didn't take a spill.

This was a perfect opportunity to press her about the accident. Or her mother. When he'd shot off a rapid-fire email to his editor, his boss had wanted any kind of information on the royals that Edward could get.

The exploding pot at the cook-off had been pure accident. But the guards—and Gideon Hale—had been on high alert during the rest of the event. Gideon and Miles had called a meeting in the bunkhouse later that night. They'd kept it vague but let the cowboys know there was a threat against Tirith's mother—and the princesses by extension.

Edward had feigned sleep in his bunk until all the other hands were snoring. He'd snuck outside to sit on the back stoop with the small laptop he kept hidden in his rucksack and spent hours when he could've been sleeping digging into what the threat might be.

Turned out there was more than one person who disliked the royal family enough to make threats against them.

He needed to narrow his search. And maybe tonight he could get Tirith to give him a clue what direction he should go.

His mind whirled as he walked the horse out of the stall and slowly saddled it up. He slipped the bit into the animal's mouth and buckled the bridle.

"Thank you," Tirith murmured from behind him. "I know you've worked hard today and must be ready to get some rest."

He finished with the bridle and held the reins loosely as he turned toward her.

"I've always got time for you, highness."

He saw the hint of vulnerability in her gaze before she dropped her eyes.

Had she always been so slight? Tonight she seemed to almost fold in on herself, her hands clasped on her elbows, her arms across her midsection.

For the first time, he felt a pang of guilt at his deception.

Think of Peyton.

He imagined his niece lying bandaged in a hospital bed.

But even as his imagination overlay the image of this moment, his insides twisted. This wasn't as easy as he'd thought, in his righteous anger, it would be.

He cleared his throat and extended the reins to her. "Here you go."

She took the few steps that separated them and reached out. The hand that closed over the reins was trembling.

She stared at the animal past Edward's shoulder.

She hadn't overcome her fear of the horse at all. She was determined to bulldoze through it.

When she stepped forward and would've brushed

past him, Edward reached out and stopped her. "Wait."

She was close now, close enough that he could've put his arm around her waist. Almost as close as they'd been right after the sound he'd thought was an explosion.

He gently pried the reins from her fingers and closed the tiny distance between them, stepping so he was beside her. He nudged her one step closer to the horse, took her wrist in his hand, and raised it. He pressed his right palm against the back of her left hand so that her hand was sandwiched between his and the horse's shoulder.

At this angle, they had some protection if the horse turned its head with malicious intent—not that he was expecting that to happen. Not with this docile animal.

She was holding her breath.

He let go of her hand momentarily only to replace it with his opposite hand. He stepped so he was behind her and reached for her other hand. He placed this one against the horse's neck, just beneath its mane.

He was effectively trapping her against the horse, but if she needed to move, he would let his arms fall away.

This wasn't about blocking her. He was trying something.

They stood there breathing in time with each other, with both hands pressed against the horse. The horse's skin shivered, and Tirith shivered too. He could feel her warmth, even though their bodies weren't touching. Their only point of contact was through their hands.

He angled his face toward her. He desperately wanted to close the inch between them, press his scruffy jaw to her cheek. But he didn't.

"He's just flesh and blood," he whispered. "Just like you and me."

The truth of his words knocked into him.

Tirith might be royalty, but she wasn't so different from him. He'd seen her terror at the chili cook off. If there'd been a real emergency, she could've been injured.

She had fears. Hurts. Desires. Hopes.

What was he doing? He didn't want to see her as a real person. Only a figurehead, someone who didn't care about others, who covered up their mistakes.

He felt the tension leave her, bit by bit, even as his own tension ratcheted up.

He never should've tried to get so close to her.

He was close enough to see the curve of her cheek, the tip of her nose. She blinked, and he saw her lashes move.

She turned her face toward him, tipping her head back so that she just touched his shoulder.

"Would you ride with me?" she whispered.

* * *

Tirith walked beside Edward as he led the horse out of the barn.

He hesitated for one moment near the industrial switch that would light up the corral. And then he kept going without flipping it.

Outside, the sun was at the horizon. A few minutes of sunset remained, and the Texas twilight could last for some time. There would be at least thirty minutes of riding time.

Edward bypassed the corral entirely, then finally paused and turned to her with raised eyebrows.

She nodded to his unanswered question. She was doing this.

But it was a relief not to have to do it alone.

She took a deep breath just before he boosted her into the saddle. The leather creaked underneath her, and her stomach dipped.

He watched her, one hand at her knee and the other still holding the reins. She firmed her chin and nodded. All the while, she was shaking inside.

He stepped into the stirrup and slid into the saddle behind her, his chest brushing her back as he settled into the seat.

He offered her the reins he held in his left hand, but she shook her head.

"One thing at a time."

Her voice was a little breathless. Maybe she could blame it on the horse, but really it was Edward's nearness that made her pulse thrum in her earlobes and her skin feel tight over her bones.

He kept the reins and settled his opposite hand at her waist. She couldn't tell whether he was trying to hold her away from him, keep some distance between them... or keep her close. He'd gone quiet back in the barn. Something kept her from asking why.

His legs flexed, and the horse began to move beneath them, taking a few slow steps.

"You gotta breathe," he said, close in her ear.

She was trying.

He made some kind of grunt and then said, "Maybe one of these days you'll catch me fresh outta the shower instead of after working for hours in the hot sun. Stinkin' of manure."

He was worried about that? Something warm lit inside her, something she didn't want to examine too closely. "You don't stink." She wrinkled her nose, rethinking the words. "It's simply... the smell of a successful day at work. Something to be proud of."

He laughed, the sound a short burst of amusement. "They teach you that in princess school? How to schmooze everybody you meet, no matter how lowly?"

"What's princess school?" She couldn't help smiling. But then she schooled her voice to be more serious.

"I'm not trying to schmooze you, Edward. Or charm you."

He didn't respond to that, and she choked back the words that wanted to escape. *I like you. There's something about you that draws me.*

The horse trudged along, slowly leaving the barnyard behind. Edward made some kind of clucking sound, and the horse picked up speed, though not much.

Edward rode with a quiet confidence, completely in control. She breathed in deeply, the scents of horse and Texas wildflowers a reminder of her childhood. But those memories weren't all pleasant. It was the man at her back who somehow calmed her.

"You gonna tell me why you're so scared of horses?" he asked.

She didn't like talking about it. Didn't like thinking about it.

"You sorta owe me." His words sounded both teasing and as if he'd ground them out through clenched teeth.

She sighed. "I was thrown from a horse just before my thirteenth birthday."

Before that, she'd been as horse-crazy as Maggie. They'd been raised on the back of a horse, with Father so often riding behind, just like Edward was now.

"I was on the palace grounds in Glorvaird, and the groom who was watching over me thought perhaps the horse had been stung by a bee." She'd been a capable rider. Overconfident, maybe. Sure of her own invincibility.

"And your father didn't insist you get back on the horse?"

"My father was here, on the Triple H." With Maggie. It'd been months after the two of them had been kidnapped and held for ransom. Tirith had been trying to swim through the currents of terror to find some semblance of normalcy. Maggie hadn't been able to swim at all, and Father had brought her to the ranch, the one place she felt safe.

She never spoke of the kidnapping. It had been kept from the press. Mother never spoke of it. It was as if it had been erased. Only not in her memory.

The pause had stretched too long.

"I broke my arm rather badly. Surgery, hospital, the works. It was months before my doctors approved being back on horseback."

And when she'd tried, terror had encompassed her. She'd rushed away from the horse and vomited.

"Your father didn't figure it out?" he asked.

"No. He rarely visited Glorvaird after—it happened." And when he had, they'd only had stiff, awkward visits in the palace.

She couldn't think about that without thinking about her mother, and she didn't want to think about Mother right now.

She forced a smile into her voice. "You're a good rider. Were you raised on a ranch?"

She realized she didn't know anything about Edward. She'd been selfish to this point, thinking only about the charity events and her family's expectations.

"My brother and I had lessons when we were kids." There was something in his voice, some vagueness.

"And you ended up a cowboy."

He made a non-committal grunt.

"Are you close?" she asked.

"Our parents died when we were teens. It's been the two of us ever since. At least, until he married. I have a ten-year-old niece."

He'd tensed up, but she didn't know why.

He rushed on. "My brother's wife left when my niece was small. It's been the two of them for years. I don't get to see them as often as I'd like."

It was a niggling itch that he didn't use names. But maybe he just wanted to ensure she understood who he was talking about.

"I don't see Maggie as often as I'd like," she offered. "She and Luc split their time between Glorvaird and the Triple H. Not that I'm blaming her or anything," she hurried to say. "They're newlyweds."

"What?" he asked.

"Hmm?"

"There's something you're not saying. Weren't you

—" He cut himself off. "Do you dislike your brother-in-law?"

He'd started to say one thing and then changed to something else. Why?

"Luc and I get along. We were friends before he met Maggie."

"Ah. So you've lost your sister and your friend all at once."

"I haven't lost anyone."

She hadn't. Not really. But somehow Edward had picked up on what she hadn't said.

Now his arm came around her waist. Her pulse pounded, but he only pressed the reins into her hand before she had time to protest. "Time for you to try."

The horse was still rambling along, and though adrenaline pumped through her, she was doing it.

Dusk was falling now. The moon wasn't out, and pinpricks of white stars against the velvet blue sky above decorated the night.

She knew they shouldn't stay out for long. Father had shared about the threat that had come in an e-mail and then a package delivered to the palace. She didn't want to worry her father.

But she didn't turn the horse back toward the barn. Not yet.

Riding was more familiar than she'd expected. The movement of the horse beneath her. The slight adjustments she needed with the reins. All of it came back to her in a long-dormant muscle memory.

And then she allowed herself to lean back against Edward until her head rested against the shoulder. He froze.

And then eased, adjusting slightly so that she was nestled against him.

"I needed this," she said softly. "To spend a few minutes with someone who has no agenda for me."

She felt a new tension take over his body. Had she revealed too much of herself in that simple statement?

"We should get back," he said quietly, the words a rumble against her back.

She turned her face toward him, seeking answers to his tension.

In the near-darkness she couldn't see his eyes clearly, but she could make out the planes of his jaw and the sharpness of his cheekbones.

He breathed in, every muscle she could feel against her wound tight. On a sharp exhale, he reached up to cup her cheek.

She leaned forward, and there was only a breath between their lips. A breath passed from him to her.

He held back, maybe studying her features. Why did he hesitate?

And then he made a sound low in his throat, almost a groan. It sounded of defeat.

He crossed scarce space between them and kissed her.

The ever-present connection between them sprang to life, and she felt with a deep certainty in her belly that this was right. Her heart thrummed against her breastbone like a hummingbird's wings.

The kiss began gentle and searching, but her passion seemed to ignite his, and soon she was breathing hard.

He broke the kiss, quickly turning his face away. His hand moved from her face to scrape over his lips and jaw.

"We probably shouldn't have done that," he said. He still didn't look at her.

The bottom of her stomach dropped out.

He regretted it?

Her face flamed as she guided the horse back toward the barn. There was no hesitation as she used her legs to tell the horse to speed up. Amazingly, the animal listened.

And then she was pulling up in the barnyard.

Edward dismounted first and reached for her, but she clung to the saddle horn and stepped down herself.

She couldn't look at him and stared at the saddle instead, "I'm sorry for forcing myself on you."

"Tirith."

She couldn't bear to hear what he might say, so she rushed away in the darkness toward the house.

We shouldn't have done that.

His words circled through her head on repeat.

Was he right?

She planned to return to Glorvaird after the ball. Edward was a temporary employee. She didn't even know his plans.

They came from different worlds.

But she'd started to hope that the attraction that sparked between them was real.

Apparently, she was the only one who didn't regret that incredible kiss.

Chapter Five

Edward spotted the princess as he crossed from the barn to the bunkhouse. Twenty-four hours had passed since he'd seen her last. He barely glanced toward the ranch house in the gathering dusk but caught sight of her standing beneath a stately maple nearby.

His feet changed direction to go to her before he was even conscious of doing it.

Maybe it wasn't her.

He could only see her from a distance. Her lips were moving as if she was talking. To the tree? Maybe the girl staring up into the tree branches overhead was Margaret. Or Bea. Or even Tirith's mother.

But his heart knew. It pushed blood singing through his veins as his feet carried him toward her.

He'd come to a decision after that disastrous kiss

and her softly spoken words, *someone who has no agenda for me.*

He couldn't keep lying to her. Not now that he'd seen the real Tirith. He still didn't know why she'd agreed to the cover up after the accident, but the kind-hearted princess he'd come to know would never have hurt Peyton if she could help it.

His emotions had gotten involved. His boss would tell him they were clouding his judgment, but Edward rather thought he was seeing more clearly than ever before.

He still couldn't believe she'd kissed him.

He couldn't stop thinking about it. Couldn't forget the tiny catch in her breath just before he'd claimed her mouth. The way she'd smiled against his lips, the softness of her skin...

She wasn't the monster he'd come here to expose.

He'd lied to her from the very beginning. He couldn't change what had already happened.

Carrick didn't even know that Edward had come here. Edward had had a knee-jerk reaction when he'd seen that non-disclosure. But exposing what had happened would mean exposing Peyton to media attention too.

His boss was expecting a story. He'd given himself a self-imposed deadline. Twenty-four more hours to find out who was behind the threats against Alessandra. That would have to be enough for the paper.

He probably shouldn't go to Tirith, though he was incredibly curious about why she was talking to a tree.

He definitely should keep his distance. He wanted too badly to hold her in his arms again.

He was in trouble.

But no matter how his thoughts tumbled, his steps didn't waver.

What was she saying? He wasn't close enough to hear. Her face was uplifted to the branches above her head. She didn't seem to register his approach. Where was her bodyguard? There, standing near the corner of the house with hands loose at his sides.

The man in reflective sunglasses didn't seem to care about Edward's approach.

Edward was about to call out to her when she reached her arms above her head and jumped. He watched her disappear into the green canopy.

"Tirith?" He jogged the last few steps to stand where she'd just been. He craned his neck.

She was there, crouched on a thick branch; she held onto another near her shoulders with a white-knuckled grip. She wore a similar outfit to the one she'd worn the last time he'd seen her, though she'd exchanged the cowboy boots for sneakers.

She glanced down at him, clearly terrified. And then perturbed, her lips pinching into a white line. "What do you want, Edward?"

He let his gaze take her in.

She wasn't that high. Only six inches above his head. He could reach up and touch her ankle if he dared.

He didn't.

"One wonders why you jumped into the tree if you're scared of heights."

"One should know it's none of his business," she muttered, glancing up into the canopy above.

Ah. She was angry with him. As she should be.

"Do you want to come back down?" he asked conversationally.

"No, thank you." The words spoken through gritted teeth told him in no uncertain terms that he wasn't wanted there.

"Why not?"

She was looking upward again, and Edward didn't think she was that determined to avoid looking at him. He let his own gaze wander up through the tangle of leaves until he caught sight of the skinny orange cat that usually slunk around inside the barn. It was sitting on a branch at least ten feet above Tirith's head, near the maple's trunk.

Its tail was curled around its paws, and it stared unblinking at Tirith.

"I think he's stuck."

His heart did a funny shiver in his chest as he realized the princess had followed the cat into the tree.

"I didn't realize you were a firefighter," he said evenly.

This time the look she shot him was more exasperated than fearful. "It's a myth that fireman use their ladder trucks to rescue cats in trees. It's not a good use of their resources."

He laughed. He couldn't help it. It was a little ridiculous. That cat was at least ten feet above her, and she hadn't moved an inch since his approach.

Even under her exasperated stare, the connection he felt when he got close to her flared to life. If she'd been on the ground, he might have taken her waist in his hands, pulled her close.

She felt it too, he was sure of it, because her gaze shuttered and she glanced away.

He cleared his throat. "That cat isn't stuck."

She stared up at the animal. "How do you know?"

"Cats climb things. We had a tabby when I was a kid. She would climb straight up the side of our chimney and sit on our roof. I've seen that cat in the hayloft." Which meant it must've figured out a way to climb the wooden ladder in the barn. There was no other way up.

But instead of dropping down, Tirith gripped the upper branch more tightly and tried to straighten her legs. The branch beneath her was wide, but it still wobbled.

She gasped and crouched back down.

He'd had a sudden terrifying vision of her falling just out of his reach. "Tirith. Come down." Was his voice shaky?

"My sister loves this ranch," she said through her teeth. "and every single animal on it. Even an annoying barn cat. I can't just leave him. I'm not frightened."

Why would she lie? He could see the terror in the way she clutched the branch, the white lines around her mouth, the flutter of her eyelashes.

There was something deeper going on here. Her determination almost reeked of desperation.

"The cat climbed into the tree," he said gently. "It can climb back down. We can stand here until it does. Even if it takes all night."

We. He'd used the pronoun to get her attention.

It worked.

She glanced down at him, and he saw the hurt she'd been trying to hide. It was there in the depths of her eyes. So was everything she wasn't saying.

What if it was another mistake?

Was he going to push her away again?

Why was he doing this?

He'd been the one to pronounce their kiss a mistake—after he'd engineered opportunities to pull her close.

We probably shouldn't have done that.

He'd handled things badly from the very beginning.

"I'm sorry about last night," he said. "Things got complicated, and I panicked."

"Complicated how?"

He took too long to answer. She looked off into the distance, her eyes narrowing.

The cat watched them with gleaming eyes. Edward was a little afraid it was going to pounce down on top of him.

"Complicated because... I like you."

She looked back at him, vulnerability and hope shining in her eyes. It was the vulnerability there that unmanned him.

He reached up and gently clasped her ankle in one hand. "Will you please come down?"

She finally glanced past him to the ground. Took a shaky breath. "I don't know how."

She'd pulled herself into the tree—a feat of strength—but was afraid to drop down?

She closed her eyes and shook her head slightly, clinging to that branch. He was a bit jealous of a tree; he'd like her to cling to him. "Last time I fell, I broke my arm."

"Then I won't let you fall."

Her eyes opened and connected with his. He saw the struggle she was going through. He'd hurt her once. Could she trust him?

He ignored the guilty pang inside.

She shifted slightly, and he knew her legs had to be tired of holding that crouching position.

"Sit on the branch like it's a swing. You can drop down, and I'll catch you. I promise."

* * *

"Drop down and I'll catch you."

It sounded easy when Edward said it.

But Tirith couldn't seem to let go of the branch her arms were wrapped around.

Edward's hand was warm on her ankle. She tried to tell herself she wasn't that far from the ground. If she could land on her feet, even if Edward didn't catch her, she would probably be all right.

But there was no guarantee.

Why had she chased the stupid cat up into the stupid tree?

"I know you're thinking about when you got thrown and broke your arm. You must've been lonely and bored during those months of recovery. You probably missed your dad like crazy."

How had he guessed?

Edward's eyes were warm and compassionate.

It was a reminder of what she'd wished for so long ago. For her father to be there with her. For him to look at her like that. Wrap her in his arms and tell her everything was going to be all right.

But Maggie had needed him, too, and Tirith had never told him how much she needed him on the rare phone calls she'd shared with her dad.

"I'm right here," Edward said. Edward, who wasn't going to let her fall. He'd promised. He watched her with a steadiness that comforted her.

She wanted to believe him.

He must have seen acquiescence in her expression, because he let go of her ankle. "Sit down on the branch instead of crouching. You can drop right down."

Moving felt too scary. When she'd tried to stand, the branch beneath her had swayed She'd thought she was slipping off.

Edward didn't falter. "Sitting or standing, I'm going to catch you."

She exhaled a breath that was more tremble than air. She wrapped her arm fully around the branch that was at chest level and slowly maneuvered until she was seated on the wide branch where she'd been squatting.

Edward reached up to squeeze her calf. "There we go. Now for the easy part. Let go of the branch and drop down into my arms."

She scrunched up her nose. "I have to let go?"

"'Fraid so."

She glanced back at the ornery cat who'd fooled

her and gotten her into this problem. "Did you know, this branch is more comfortable than I thought. Ralph and I can live up here. You can bring me food and water."

His eyebrows rose. "Ralph?"

"He looks like a Ralph, doesn't he?" She nudged her head toward the cat.

His eyes were warm and if she focused only on them, she could ignore the dizziness that wanted to distract her. He looked tired. Worn out.

He tugged on the tip of her sneaker. "Come on, highness. Let go." There was warm affection in his voice instead of the sarcasm she'd heard that first day.

He took a half-step back so he wasn't directly underneath her. He held out his hands.

She let go of the branch above her and pushed herself slightly forward. She slipped off her seat on the lower branch.

She saw surprise in his eyes, but he caught her against him as she fell, her belly against his chest. His arms came around her waist, and then he set her on her feet. He steadied her with his hands at her waist.

"That was fast. After all your dawdling, I was expecting you to count to three. Or three hundred." One corner of his mouth tipped up, but his eyes were serious.

She tipped her chin. "Princesses don't dawdle. A princess is always perfectly on time."

"Ah. My mistake."

His teasing words were a reminder of the way they'd ended things last night. Awkwardness descended. He let go of her waist and stepped back.

She lowered her gaze and murmured, "Thank you for the rescue."

She expected him to make some excuse and return to the bunkhouse, but his hand clasped hers.

"Do princesses sit on the grass without a picnic blanket?" He didn't wait for an answer, just tugged her toward the base of the tree. She sat, and he lowered beside her, shoulder-to-shoulder.

He tilted his head up to see the furry animal in the branches above. "How'd you end up out here anyway?"

She didn't know if he was talking to the cat or to her. "I'm supposed to be cataloguing the last-minute entries for Maggie's silent auction. I just... needed a break."

Mother had come to check on her one too many times. It was stifling, being in the same room with her, with so many things unsaid. And heaven forbid Father be inside the house at the same time Mother was.

Tirith leaned her head back against the trunk. She closed her eyes. "You were right," she said quietly. "I did miss my father after I broke my arm." *I still miss him.* She swallowed back the unhelpful words. "I never asked him to come see me, though. So it's partly my fault."

It took a moment before Edward responded, his voice low. "Why not?"

"Because Maggie needed him."

Just the fact that he'd stayed, that he was keeping his promise to wait for the silly cat with her, made something open up deep inside her.

"Just before our twelfth birthday, Maggie and I were kidnapped from under our bodyguard's protection." She'd never told anybody that before.

Edward went tense beside her and his hand seemed to tighten involuntarily on hers.

"It didn't last long," she said quickly. "And we weren't harmed. Just frightened. After... Maggie couldn't handle being in Glorvaird. Making appearances. Being in crowds. Father brought her back here, to the Triple H, where she felt safe."

"What about you?" There was a harshness in his voice. "Where did you feel safe?"

"On my horse," she whispered. The silver gelding had been so fast... fast enough to race away if someone came too close.

"Only that turned out to be dangerous, too," he murmured.

He saw through her too easily.

She tilted her head upward. Checked on the cat. Still there.

Edward angled toward her. He brushed a strand of hair from where it was caught in her eyelashes. He was close, his gaze both tender and probing.

"Hey," he whispered.

She smiled. There was something about his presence that made those painful memories fade.

His fingers slid across her cheek, his touch soft and seeking. His fingers slid into her hair, tipping her head back slightly.

"What are you doing?" she breathed against his lips.

"Complicating things." And then his lips closed over hers, and she didn't have time to wonder what he meant.

He kept the kiss gentle and light, filled with such tenderness that it warmed her from the inside out, filling up all the cracks from her broken childhood.

When he turned his head and eased back from the kiss, her stomach twisted. But he only settled her closer against him, his arm around her shoulders.

He glanced up into the tree. Apparently the cat was still there.

"And your mother?"

It took a moment for her to register his question, remember what they were talking about.

"Did she help you through those months?"

Usually, thinking about her mother brought on so many difficult feelings. But with her head leaning against Edward's shoulder, she only felt a ghost of the usual swirl of emotions.

"Mother was in the middle of a long and difficult trade negotiation with one of our neighboring countries. She was often at home, but she was so busy…"

He pressed a kiss to her temple. "And?"

"And I didn't want to be a bother. I told myself I was fine."

Only she wasn't. She hadn't been fine in a long time.

"I started having panic attacks when I was fifteen. I didn't know what was happening at first. And then… I hid it. Anxiety isn't a very royal emotion. The attacks got worse. And then, two years ago, I—"

She blinked away memories of the flashing emergency lights, of Peyton's crumpled body.

She'd caused that.

This was the moment. Talking about her fragile mental state made her terribly uncomfortable, and she felt the discomfort seeping in now.

She edged away from Edward, but he caught her hand and twined their fingers together. "Tirith. Whatever you tell me won't go any farther."

She turned her face away, hiding from him. Shame suffused her. "I've only spoken about it to my therapist."

She was still working through the muddle that was her life. A part of her wanted to get up. Put some physical distance between Edward and this difficult conversation. He must've felt the slight way she turned from him. Barely a movement at all.

"If you can't tell me, then just... stay."

Did he care? Because she was starting to fall for him. And if she stayed, her heart would only get more tangled up.

She settled back against him, ignoring the way her derrière was going numb sitting on the hard ground.

She'd managed to tell Edward about her panic attacks, her anxiety, and he wanted to stay close to her.

Maybe it was dangerous to allow her heart to get involved with him. They were certainly different. She didn't know where he would go after his time on the Triple H was done.

But when she was with him, she felt... at peace. As if she could, one day, like herself again.

Chapter Six

I *never meant to hurt you.*

Edward ran the words through again and again as he sidled up to the horse secured in its trailer and untied its lead.

He had to tell Tirith the truth. Why he'd come. That he'd had a change of heart.

That he'd lied to her.

His plans to dig into the threat against Alessandra and leave had changed after Tirith's heartfelt confessions under the maple tree. He didn't want any negative attention pointed toward her or her family.

She wasn't a monster. She was a woman trying to deal with the trauma in her own past.

His cell phone buzzed in his pocket. He glanced at it and refused the call. He couldn't talk to Holly right now. His boss would be furious that Edward had spent weeks on this story and would have nothing to show for it.

He had morals. Professional ethics.

And what Tirith was going through was nobody's business but hers.

But sometime over the past few days, he'd begun to want to be a part of her life. To be the one she shared her hurts with.

He didn't know if that would be possible once he told her the truth of his identity.

But he had to try.

He used the horse's halter to lead it down the ramp before he tied it off on the side of the trailer.

There was noise and activity all around. The parking area where all the horse trailers were congregated was packed with trucks and horses and competitors preparing for the rodeo. Barrel racers and ropers were settling their horses. He'd seen one teen girl giving her horse's tail a fancy braid.

He had to admit he'd been a little starstruck by some of the famous rodeo names the royal family had managed to wrangle into this event.

Edward hefted the fancy saddle and began to secure it, aware of the heavy boot steps approaching from around the truck.

Gideon Hale's strident voice rang out, calling out the false name Edward had given. "Bouchard."

Edward had had a recurring nightmare about the

ex-operator discovering his identity and making him disappear forever. The man was probably just checking up on his daughter's horse.

Edward worked to keep his voice even and unaffected. "Mr. Hale. What can I do for you?"

"You can leave my daughter alone."

Edward glanced only briefly at Hale, long enough to see the black vest over his dress jeans and fancy felt hat. Was he entering an event? Edward kept working on the currycomb, running his free hand over the horse's shoulder and side. "I'm not sure what you're talking about."

Gideon stepped closer, forcing Edward to drop the currycomb and focus on him. "Don't play games with me."

Not good. "What game?"

Hale's stare was hard. "Do you want to tell me who you really are?"

Everything inside Edward went still. Had Hale found him out? What did he know? Edward hadn't been grabbed and escorted bodily off the premises. Maybe Hale was simply bluffing?

The horse stamped one of its front hooves, obviously picking up on the tension Edward was attempting to hide. Hale knew horses. Edward was going to have to do a better job if he didn't want to be found out right this second.

Edward showed his teeth. Not quite a smile.

"I'm Edward." He left off his last name. No use lying now, not when he didn't know how deep Hale had dug.

"That's the name you gave us, but the more I look into you, the more your background seems a little too put-together to be real."

Edward's pulse was still pounding, but his thoughts were clear. Hale was guessing, fishing for information.

Edward had been on the *asking questions* side of the interrogator's table enough times that he knew the best thing he could do was stay calm. Miles had tasked him with readying Tirith's horse. So he kept on securing her saddle, tightening the girth, buckling the stirrup into place.

"Why're you so interested in me?"

Hale didn't hesitate. "Because you seem to be interested in my daughter."

Where had the man's protective nature been when Tirith had been a hurting teen? When she'd needed her father's comfort and he'd been absent? Edward wanted to push for answers to those questions, though he knew he didn't have the right.

Edward had barely finishing securing the saddle when Hale grabbed his shoulder and spun him around so they were face-to-face. Edward worked to hold on to his temper even as Gideon stared at him with hard, glittering eyes.

The horse's tail swished. Its ears twitched on high alert.

"There are some really nasty people who've threatened my family. If one of them decided to try and get close, masquerading as a ranch hand would be a good way to do it."

"I don't want to hurt your family."

The words tasted like ash in his mouth. Edward had come here intending to do just that. He'd planned for Tirith to be humiliated, her family exposed when he'd uncovered what she'd done to Peyton. He'd arrived on the Triple H full of self-righteousness.

And then he had gotten to know Tirith.

He had let himself get confused. Peyton and Carrick deserved justice. But if what Tirith said was true, if her inattention had been due to a panic attack, as he suspected, and not negligence, that changed everything. And she'd tried to make things right by paying Peyton's medical bills, if he'd understood what the NDA and Carrick's emails meant.

Hale somehow saw Edward's whirling thoughts. Or maybe he just sensed blood in the water. "If you aren't one of the Bello family's minions, then what are you? A reporter?"

The accusation hit too close to home. Edward worked to keep his expression neutral. "Why? Do you have skeletons in your closet? You got some reason for staying separated from your wife all these years?"

He knew the words were a mistake as soon as they left his lips.

Hale grabbed the collar of his shirt, and Edward braced for a punch.

It didn't come.

"I want you out of here," Hale said, voice dangerously low. "Off the Triple H tonight. You can check in with Miles at the ranch house and pick up your pay."

Edward started to protest, but before he could get a word out, Tirith rounded the back of the trailer.

Hale let go of Edward so fast that he almost stumbled.

Confusion passed over Tirith's expressive face. "What's going on?"

"Nothing," Hale answered firmly. He shot a look at Edward, who considered blurting out, *Your father just fired me!* But that would sound like sour grapes. And then he registered her outfit.

She wore a vest of the colors of the Glorvaird flag over a bright white shirt with sequins down the outside of each sleeve. Her hair had been fussed and sprayed into a traditional Texas style that made him smile. Her face was too made up, probably so her features would be visible under the harsh lights of the stadium. She wore fancy jeans with blue sequins down the side of them too and red cowboy boots.

He'd never seen a more beautiful rodeo cowgirl.

And he couldn't ruin her moment. Not when she was nervous about getting on the back of the horse.

"Daddy, what—?"

"We're fine." Edward brushed past Hale. When the man would've stopped him, he raised his chin and glared.

"You look beautiful, highness." He brushed a kiss against her cheek. "I'll see you later."

Let Hale think he was complying.

Things weren't finished between him and Tirith. He needed to talk to her. Find a way to tell her the truth. Find a way to be in her life.

But this was her moment. And he wouldn't take it from her.

* * *

She couldn't do this.

Tirith stood next to Ace's head, holding the horse's reins with shaking hands. After Edward had disappeared, Father had helped her check the horse's cinch and bridle and left her with Maggie at the bustling area outside the arena gate.

Maggie was already seated on her horse several yards away, chatting with a girl who held a Texas state flag. Maggie's United States flag was secured in its special leather rig attached to the saddle.

Tirith eyed the Glorvaird flag attached to her own

saddle. It didn't seem to bother the horse. All she had to do was hold it steady with one hand. Hold the reins in the other.

It would be just like riding around the corral at home.

Except it wasn't the same at all.

Flood lights illuminated the stadium. The stands were packed. Maggie should be proud of herself. This was a great turnout.

Tirith didn't know where Father had disappeared to. Maybe checking on Mother and Bea, who were watching from the viewing box installed on the far end of the arena, near where the announcer was stationed. There'd been words exchanged between them earlier. Father still didn't want Mother to be out in such a public setting.

Mother hadn't raised her voice, had used only stilted and polite words, but she'd scoffed at Father's worry and told him in no uncertain terms that she would attend Maggie's rodeo.

Tirith had been on the other side of Mother's cold dismissal just that morning when she'd brought up her proposal again.

Anxiety rose inside her, choking off her breath.

Mother thought Tirith was going to muck things up. Maybe she was right.

"You okay there? Need help mounting up?"

She shook her head as she waved off the friendly

cowboy who'd approached. What she needed was a time machine so she could go back and tell Maggie she wasn't doing this.

It didn't matter that she'd ridden the horse around the corral all on her own yesterday. There hadn't been a thousand pairs of eyes watching her yesterday.

She caught Maggie's worried gaze and tried to smile. She turned away quickly, afraid her expression had looked more like a grimace.

All of a sudden, the chatter around her seemed to quiet. Was she having an all-out panic attack?

No.

Everyone had mounted up.

It was time to go in there.

Tirith attempted to swallow her fear. She slipped her foot in the stirrup and pulled herself into the saddle. The leather creaked beneath her weight. Her horse blew and shook its head as it felt the tension she was holding in her back. It took one step to the right.

She wasn't going to be able to keep the horse under control. What had she been thinking? She was going to get thrown.

From her perch on the horse's back, she had a better view of the crowd.

She squinted against the bright stadium lights. Earlier when she'd seen Edward near the horse trailer, he'd been wearing a blue-and-white checked shirt with silver snaps. Under the black cowboy hat, his jaw showed two days' worth of stubble.

A man sitting in the third row of the stadium seats could've passed for his doppelgänger.

As she watched, his stare zeroed in on her. It *was* Edward!

He nodded at her, his mouth hinting at the curve of a smile.

I'll catch you.

Edward believed in her. He'd listened to her, encouraged her.

Even if her nerves got her tossed from the horse, he'd be there to scoop her up.

She forced herself to relax the hand that held the horse's reins. She exhaled a long breath and some of her jangling nerves.

The wide gates into the arena were opened by two long-legged cowboys, and she heard a deep voice over the loudspeaker, though she couldn't make out the words. And then Maggie was beside her.

"You ready?" Maggie asked.

Tirith reached out her left hand and steadied the flag pole attached to her saddle. She glanced past her sister to catch Edward's eye once more. "Let's go."

She lost sight of Edward, concentrating on getting the horse into the brightly lit arena the way she and Maggie had practiced earlier in the day on foot. Tirith stayed on the inside, with Maggie at her right, a half step ahead.

She was doing it.

Her chin lifted in triumph as she rode past the glass-enclosed box where her mother must be sitting. *Look at me. I'm all right.*

She was going to push her proposal past Mother. Earn the approval of her aunt, the ruling monarch. Maybe even later tonight.

There was one terrifying moment when Maggie kicked her horse into a trot. They hadn't practiced that, but her sister sent her a look with her eyebrows lifted. A dare. Tirith was rusty in the saddle, but she wasn't going to let her sister best her.

She posted up and asked her horse for a trot. Her form must look terrible compared to Maggie's, but the faster pace allowed the flags to unfurl behind them in all their glory.

And then it was over.

Tirith's cheeks were aching from smiling so widely as she followed Maggie out of the arena. The other riders who had paraded in the arena behind them crowded around, and she felt a moment of nervousness as her horse shifted beneath her. Maggie tipped her head, and Tirith followed her out of the chaos into a holding area closer to where all the horse trailers were parked.

Both sisters dismounted, and Maggie reached for

Tirith's reins. Tirith might have overcome her fear, but she was content to let her sister take the horse. Maggie nodded to someone behind Tirith. She turned to see that Edward was there, striding toward her.

She was so intensely happy that she threw herself at him, not caring who watched. He caught her with his hands at her waist while her arms went around his neck.

She was exultant. A laugh rang out of her throat.

She had done it.

She gazed up into his face and knew that everything she was feeling must be written on her face, but for once she didn't care. She saw recognition in his eyes and the warm affection that followed. He tipped his head toward her. She lifted her chin for his kiss.

But her father's strident voice broke through the haze of her joy. "Tirith."

And then, "I told you to stay away from my daughter."

Edward's hands fell away from her waist. She was forced to step back as Father invaded Edward's personal space.

She hadn't understood the scene near her horse trailer earlier, but she'd had only minutes before her ride into the arena. She hadn't had time for questions. She didn't understand the tension between the two men now.

"What is going on?" she demanded.

Father's gaze turned to her, and her stomach dropped at the fierceness in his expression. "Your *friend* here is a journalist." His disgusted tone said exactly what he thought of Edward's friendship.

The bottom of her stomach dropped out. A journalist? It couldn't be true.

Father turned back to Edward. "One of my contacts sent over your file ten minutes ago."

There was guilt written clearly on Edward's face even as his eyes pleaded with her.

"Edward?" Her voice sounded far away to her own ears.

"Let me explain."

But Father was pushing him away from her. "I told you to stay away from my daughter. You've got two minutes to vacate this property."

A bulky bodyguard was closing in behind Father.

She was frozen in place, both hot and cold at the same time.

Maggie was there, her hand at Tirith's elbow.

Maggie.

Tirith had told Edward about Maggie. About the kidnapping. About her resentment, her sorrow. The panic attacks.

Coldness slipped over her body like an icy blanket. There were people all around, voices and curious stares. This felt surreal, as if she was watching from outside her body.

Edward had lied to her.

His eyes were almost wild as he stared at her.

"Tirith, it's not what you think. Just give me five minutes."

She couldn't give him that. She couldn't bear to see him any longer.

She closed her eyes and let Maggie lead her away.

Edward called out after her. She heard a scuffle as he must've tried to follow. She couldn't look back.

What had she done?

She started to say something, apologize to Maggie, but the sound that emerged was more moan that words.

Maggie shushed her. "We'll figure everything out. Just not right this moment."

This was Maggie's moment. Maggie's fundraiser.

And Tirith had caused enough chaos for one evening.

She opened her eyes. Squeezed her sister's arm. "You've got to get ready for your ride." The barrel racing portion of the evening would begin soon, and Maggie was the crowd favorite.

Maggie watched her with concern, compassion clear in the depths of her eyes. Maybe she hadn't understood. She hadn't been standing near when Father had revealed Edward's occupation.

Or maybe she understood too well. They'd always had an uncanny knack at reading each other's feelings.

"I'm fine," Tirith insisted. She wasn't. She might not ever be again. "I'll join Mother in the box." It was the last place she wanted to be but probably the safest place on the property.

No doubt Mother would have something to say about what Tirith had done. She'd let a journalist get close to her, uncover family secrets. It wasn't the scandal Mother had been worried about, but it was another strike against Tirith.

Maybe Mother was right. Maybe she wasn't the right person to head up a new royal initiative.

She was a disaster.

Chapter Seven

Edward didn't know what he'd expected, but it wasn't to see Peyton sitting cross-legged on the floor across from a young woman in scrubs. His niece was giggling at something the woman had said.

She looked so... normal.

Edward hung back in the hallway, his brother's living room open before him as he watched his niece. He'd used his key—Carrick might take it away after Edward had a frank conversation with him tonight—to gain access to his brother's Glorvaird apartment. His flight had landed late enough in the evening that he'd thought Peyton would be in bed.

Apparently, he was wrong.

She was taller than he remembered. It had been months since he'd been home.

Too long.

Peyton was growing up, and he was missing it. She still looked as sweet as ever, with the spray of freckles across her face and her lashes making dark fans against her cheeks when she looked down.

She was still Peyton.

His heart swelled with love for his niece. He backed up a step, not wanting to interrupt. When he glanced down the hallway, Carrick was watching him from his office doorway.

Carrick's expression was closed-off, his gaze cool. He nodded farther down the hallway, and Edward moved silently into the kitchen. His brother followed.

"You mind if I make some coffee?" Edward asked, voice low, not wanting to disrupt Peyton and her helper.

"Fine." Carrick's shortness was probably merited. Edward had shown up out of the blue.

He needed to find the right words to apologize, but he was exhausted and heartsick.

He hadn't had a chance to speak to Tirith. Last night, he'd been escorted not just off the Triple H, but all the way to the airport. His burly, armed escort had followed him until he'd boarded the plane. Destination: London. Apparently, Gideon Hale's contact had discovered everything about Edward, including his home address. Edward had caught a flight from there directly to Glorvaird.

During his layover, he'd tried to call Tirith, but she'd blocked his number. His texts had never been delivered.

He hadn't slept.

He couldn't stop thinking about the shock and betrayal he'd seen on her expression before she'd carefully blanked her features.

He'd tried to get to her, but her father had blocked his way and then physically restrained him. Edward had gotten a punch in the stomach and his arm twisted behind his back before she'd been out of sight and he'd gone limp. Given up.

He'd hurt her with his lies. His quest for revenge.

During the airplane ride, he'd tried to imagine a way that he could see her.

This couldn't be the end for them.

She'd return to Glorvaird after the charity ball. Maybe he could make an official request to see her through the palace. Unless she refused him.

His exhausted brain hadn't been able to come up with any good ideas.

Because he knew he didn't deserve a second chance. Or her forgiveness. He wouldn't blame her if she never wanted to see him again.

Right now he needed to focus on Carrick and Peyton.

The single-cup coffee maker had stopped its drip, and he took the mug and faced his brother.

"What are you doing here?" Carrick looked tired. Lines fanned his eyes, and his shirt was rumpled. Edward felt a beat of guilt. He should've come sooner, been here to help his brother.

"I... did something stupid."

Carrick crossed his arms over his chest and waited for Edward to go on.

"I came home to see you guys. About two months ago."

He'd surprised Carrick with that information. Probably because he hadn't actually seen either of them. "I got in really late. I knew you were at the hospital, so I stopped in to sleep for a few hours." He'd planned to join them at the hospital first thing in the morning. "I had a thought for an article I didn't want to forget and went into your office to find a pen. Your computer was booted up. Your email was open."

Carrick's eyes flashed fire. "You snooped through my emails?"

Edward met his angry stare head-on, coffee forgotten. "I saw the royal seal and I..." *Couldn't help myself.* He didn't say that. He could've. He'd just chosen to override his good sense. "I invaded your privacy."

Carrick turned to face the cabinetry. He gripped the counter and dropped his head. "I signed an NDA. You broke into my computer, got into my private emails, but I guess it's still my fault. I should've had it password protected."

"That's not all of it."

Carrick's head came up, and Edward flinched at the fury in his expression. "Please tell me you did *not* write something—" He cut himself off, shaking his head. "Of course you wrote something."

Edward's throat was dry, but he forced the words out. "I went to America. To confront the royal family. I made a mistake. They know I'm a journalist and it won't take much for them to link me to you." Saying the words brought back the memory, not of those terrible final moments together, but of Tirith's quiet trust when she'd shared with him about the kidnapping, about a young girl who'd missed her dad. She'd shared her deepest wound with him.

Carrick slammed one hand on the counter, apparently no longer trying to be quiet. "How could you? Do you know how exorbitant Peyton's hospital bills are? Every bill for her care has been paid for"—he lowered his voice, apparently remembering they weren't alone in the apartment—"by the royal family. But only if I honor the NDA." He let loose a stream of curse words that Edward had never heard his usually-reserved brother say. "Where am I going to get the funds to pay it all back?"

Carrick's anger had morphed into desperation.

Edward's chest felt tight. He'd done this. Pushed Carrick to the point of tears with worry over his little girl. "I'm sorry." The words were so inadequate. "I'll pay whatever it takes." He had a small nest egg saved up, and his apartment in London. He could sell that, though his equity wouldn't be enough to pay *exorbitant* hospital bills.

"I don't want your money." Carrick's voice had gone cold. He stared at the wall, not even looking at Edward. "And Peyton and I don't need someone like you in our lives."

The words cut like a knife. Edward had come here to make things right, but he'd only hurt Carrick. Hurt Peyton. His eyes burned. "I'm sorry."

Carrick shook his head, still unable to look at Edward. "You've always been more dedicated to your job than our relationship. I don't know why I'm surprised that you'd do this."

Edward flinched as if he had been struck. "That's not true." His words were an instinctive denial.

"You missed my high school graduation because you were too busy playing journalist." Carrick didn't even have to think about the accusation. The words were quick cuts, as if he'd played the duel of this part of the conversation over and over.

The old grief expanded in Edward's chest, joining the other constant pain. "That's not why."

Was Carrick even listening?

Edward rushed on, afraid his brother was about to throw him out of the apartment. "After Dad died, I could barely keep your tuition current." Carrick had needed consistency. At least that's what Edward had believed. He'd thought the Glorvaird boarding school would provide it. And Edward had been sent on assignment all the time. He was gone more than he was home. "I wrote sixteen hours a day." He'd freelanced on top of his journalist work, writing for any publication that would pay him. "You couldn't go on to university without your transcript, and I knew they wouldn't release it if your tuition was unpaid."

Carrick peered at Edward now, his eyes flashing disbelief.

"It killed me not to be there. I made the best choice I could." His boss at the time had been particularly hard-nosed. Edward had been on assignment. If he'd left to attend Carrick's graduation, he would've been fired. And then he wouldn't have been able to pay the tuition.

"Why didn't you say anything?"

"Say anything like what? We were both in survival mode."

Carrick's voice was choked with emotion. "If you had just told me that you wanted to be there. Just a phone call to let me know that you cared, I wouldn't have felt so alone."

Carrick had felt this way for years? This was what had driven the wedge between them?

Edward didn't know how to cross the gulf between

them. But he had to try. "I wanted to be there. For all of it."

Carrick stared at him with a grim frown. Maybe Edward's emotional declaration was too little, too late.

And then Carrick's expression crumpled. "I needed you. I need you. But not as some avenging angel. Peyton and I need you in our lives every day."

Edward's throat was hot and tight. Was Carrick giving him a second chance?

* * *

Tirith knew she shouldn't, but she hit the spacebar on her computer, and the footage played again.

She recognized the interior of the 4-H building, the setup for the chili cook-off. But this clip wasn't edited like the pieces that had been added to Maggie's charity website.

Maggie had sent it to her directly. It was a rough cut of the excruciating moments when she'd touched her face after chopping that darned jalapeño pepper.

She zeroed in on Edward. He scowled directly into the computer screen. *"Turn the camera off. You can come back to us later."*

And then he pulled her to his chest. She remembered that moment. Remembered the way her eyes stung and watered so badly, remembered the feeling of safety when he'd tucked her into him.

Right now she couldn't stop staring at his face, recorded for eternity. The way he looked at her puffy, tearing face...

That wasn't the sly look of a man who was using her for his own gain.

He looked at her like... like she was something precious. As if he was surprised to find a treasure in his hands.

She blinked and glanced up from the screen, not really taking in the sleek hotel suite's sitting room around her. She closed the laptop, wishing she could close off her roiling emotions just as easily. She needed to clear her head. She was expecting company. Why had Maggie sent this clip to her?

Late into the night after the rodeo, there'd been a family meeting—with the PR team from the palace joining via video—and Tirith had been forced to confess to all of it. Her growing friendship with Edward. The things she'd confided to him.

She'd kept her true feelings to herself, not willing to divulge to her judgmental mother just how deeply she'd fallen for Edward's con. But later that night, Maggie had come to her room, and Tirith hadn't been able to keep the truth inside any longer. She'd told Maggie everything. How Edward had charmed her. How he'd listened. How her feelings for him had grown.

Maggie had told her that she hadn't done anything

wrong by opening her heart. It was Edward who had lied to her.

The knowledge he'd gained was a PR nightmare.

But two days after the rodeo, not a hint of it had hit the media. Was Edward simply biding his time?

Her heart wanted to believe that because no story had appeared in the news, it meant Edward hadn't betrayed her.

Maggie's video clip was making the confusion worse.

Tirith couldn't afford to hope. Whatever relationship she'd believed was unfolding with Edward was fiction. She'd needed to show her mother that she was capable of running this new initiative.

And then the fiasco with Edward had happened.

She'd only begun to believe in herself again.

And this thing with Edward—as awful as it was—couldn't take that away.

A soft knock on the door brought her out of her thoughts. Her cousin Valentin stuck his head inside. "Can I come in?"

"Of course." She stood to receive the hug he offered.

She and Val had become close after Maggie and Dad had left Glorvaird. They'd commiserated over living under their mothers' thumbs in the palace.

She was ashamed that she'd let their friendship

fade after the accident. She hadn't wanted to share her struggle with him.

It was time she took back her life.

"Thank you for meeting with me," she murmured as they sat on adjacent sofas. He didn't settle into the furniture but sat forward with his elbows loosely on his knees, giving her his full attention.

"Crystal will be sorry she missed the chance to see you."

His fiancée, Crystal, was a delight. They would have to catch up later.

"I know you don't have long to chat," she started.

She was surprised when he reached out and put his hand over hers. "I have as long as you need. What's up?"

Tears smarted. What had she done to be so blessed by the family she had?

"I want to start a new royal initiative. A charity, maybe."

She saw his slight hesitation and guessed at the cause. "I've spoken to my mother, but she's worried about the image of the royal family." Mother's thoughts on this subject were outdated and wrong. Still, Tirith needed to finesse this conversation.

Valentin nodded for her to go on.

"Have you ever been close to someone who suffers from anxiety or depression?" Her chest tightened at the question. She wasn't used to speaking so openly about this. But she'd learn to grow comfortable.

Valentin considered her. "I don't know. Have I?"

Her cousin was perceptive. His steady, compassionate manner made it easier for her to find the words to tell him about what she'd been through. About the things she'd learned about herself, how she'd grown, where she still needed support.

He listened to all of it, including her ideas on how the royal family should be speaking out against the stigma of mental illness. She told him her preliminary plans and where she wanted to go with the charity.

By the time she was finished, Val had cast off his suit jacket and loosened his tie. He sat back in the sofa with one leg crossed over his knee. One hand rested across the back of the furniture while the other hand tapped against its arm. He was deep in thought, considering every angle.

"This is important work," he said.

The last little bit of tension she'd held as she'd explained herself was whisked away. Her cousin, her dear friend, understood. Even when Mother couldn't.

"I'll speak to my mother," he said, "but her agreement isn't necessary for you to start your work. If you'll write up a proposal, I can present it during the next council meeting."

Her eyes blurred with tears as she moved across the space to hug her cousin.

He patted her back and then let her ease back into her seat.

Valentin's acceptance would help her get one step closer to the goal she'd set for herself. She was both elated and filled with nervous anticipation. Now, she must get to work.

After the charity ball in two days.

And maybe throwing herself into this work would help her forget about Edward.

Chapter Eight

This was it.

Tirith stood at the top of a wide stair-case, the expansive ballroom laid out before her. Men in tuxedos, women in dresses of every color. The guests mingled and chatted.

And watched as the members of the royal family were announced. Including Tirith.

She had imagined this moment numerous times over the past few weeks. In some of her most far-fetched dreams, she had pictured herself standing at the top of this elegant staircase on Edward's arm.

But she was here alone.

And she was going to have to learn to be content with that.

She had her family.

She and Maggie had dressed together, both of

them giggling the way they had when they'd been young girls.

Val had promised Tirith a dance after he took a turn around the parquet floor with his fiancée. He'd already spoken with his mother about Tirith's new charity. Tirith would hit the ground running when she returned to Glorvaird.

She and her father had finally cleared the air about those lost years after the kidnapping. Dad had apologized for not being there when she'd needed him. Admitting her feelings hadn't been that bad. They were already finding a way back to the closeness they'd once shared.

This solitude wouldn't last forever.

Her elegant designer gown swirled around her when she took her place at the top of the stairs after she'd been announced. Her gaze caught on the two massive chandeliers overhanging the ballroom. They were huge works of art, curls of metal and crystal.

There was applause from the assembled guests and, for one breathless moment, she thought she saw Edward's dark-haired figure among the crowd.

She was being ridiculous.

Edward wasn't a knight in shining armor. She didn't *need* a knight in shining armor.

She had herself.

She smiled as cameras flashed, the approved media

wearing noticeable name tags on lanyards around their necks.

She barely felt the stab of hurt at the thought of another member of the press.

She moved downstairs and was mingling with the crowd when she caught sight of Maggie several yards away. Her sister's eyes were huge, and not with excitement. Why did she look anxious? She made a motion with her hand that Tirith couldn't decipher. A tall man interrupted Tirith's view of her sister, and the press of people obscured her.

Tirith made her excuses, intending to go find Maggie, when the crowd parted.

All of a sudden, she came face to face with Edward.

He was wearing a tailored tuxedo with a black bowtie, and he was so intensely handsome with his chiseled jaw shaved clean and those piercing eyes that she stumbled. She stared openly at him, unable to comprehend what was happening.

Other people swirled around then, moving around in the ballroom. But she was frozen.

"Hello, Tirith."

How did he have the brain function needed to speak? Her heart was pounding. She didn't think she could form words.

"Can we talk?" His expression read grim.

"I have nothing to say to you."

She spoke the words she was expected to say—she wouldn't share anything with him, not when he had the power to hurt her family—but it cost her. Oh, how it cost her.

And he saw it too. She saw the echo of her hurt in the twist of his lips.

She couldn't do this. Couldn't face him in this public space and keep her composure.

She spun on her heel, frantically searching the periphery of the room for an escape.

But he caught her elbow in his hand. "Tirith, please. Just for a moment."

She wouldn't cry out, wouldn't give him the satisfaction of causing a scene. She glanced over her shoulder at him. Where was his press badge? Had he been able to waltz right in the front door?

She didn't have a chance to pull her elbow from his grasp.

There was a loud *pop*. Then another.

Several voices in the crowd cried out.

A distinct ripping sound overhead had both Tirith and Edward instinctively looking up.

One of the massive glass-and-metal chandeliers was swaying.

Before she knew what was happening, Edward pushed her out of the way. She tripped on the wide skirt of her dress and fell flat to the ground. She lost her breath.

Edward covered her body with his.

There was an explosion of sound, metal against metal. Glass shattered.

When she peered under her arm, she saw that the chandelier had crashed to the ground.

Someone was shrieking, but the sound seemed muted.

Edward's warm hand clasped her bare upper arm. He helped her scramble to her feet. "Are you all right?"

Her heartbeat was pounding in her temples. She couldn't quite take stock of her body.

"Tirith."

He moved back slightly just as there was another *pop*. She flinched.

Was that a gunshot?

One of Father's guards ushered her toward the wall. "We've got to move."

She grabbed for Edward. He pressed closely against her back even as the guard kept her right behind him, so she was sandwiched between their two bodies.

Who would shoot into a crowded ballroom?

It seemed to take forever, but only a few seconds had passed by the time the guard ushered her and Edward into a utilitarian hallway.

They kept moving. Where was Maggie? Bea, Val, Mother, Father?

She couldn't breathe.

Why hadn't the guard separated her from Edward? She thought of those terrible gunshots and reached behind her blindly. Edward seemed to understand she needed reassurance because his hand closed over hers. His other arm came around to brace her shoulder.

The guard unlocked and threw open a door, his gun aimed in front of him as he peered inside. He motioned for her and Edward to enter. He stood inside the door, peering out. He seemed to be listening to his earpiece.

He glanced back at Tirith, who waited with bated breath.

"There's conflicting information coming across. It seems everyone is secure. But your father is requesting backup. Stay here until someone brings the car around."

Before she could ask why Father needed backup, the guard was gone. He'd said everyone was secure. That meant safe, didn't it?

She struggled to remember the layout of the facility. Her father's team had gone over everything in a security briefing this morning, but she hadn't paid enough attention. Like Mother, she hadn't believed the threat was real.

She'd gotten turned around in the chaos of the ballroom, but it was obvious this was a storage area. The room was full of stacks of extra chairs. Round tables were leaning against the walls on both sides with a narrow walkway left between. At the end, she saw part of a doorway, the lighted exit sign above it.

And she and Edward were alone under the stark fluorescent lights.

"Are you all right?" He dropped her hand and stepped back, his eyes scanning over her.

"I don't know."

She started shivering. When had it become so icy cold in the building? Only moments before, she'd been overheated in the ballroom.

He noticed, of course. Edward noticed everything.

He brushed his thumb over her cheek. "You've got a small scratch here. Probably from the flying glass."

But it would've been much worse if he hadn't shoved her out of the way. She might've been crushed by the chandelier.

He'd blocked her body from the flying glass and metal. The elbow of his tuxedo jacket was ripped, and his hair had a sparkle like he'd picked up glass shards.

He shrugged out of his jacket and threw it out around her shoulders. She let the warmth close over her, breathed in deeply of his familiar scent. She put her trembling hands through the sleeves.

He seemed satisfied that she would be all right for the moment. He paced toward the exit door and then back, glancing all around as if he might find a secret passageway. He stopped several feet away. "What is this room?"

"What are you doing here?" she blurted. "And where is your press badge?"

He had the audacity to smile at her. "I'm not here as a member of the press."

"How did you get in? My father—"

"Your father is pretty scary. But I explained to him exactly why I needed to see you, and he relented. He gave me one chance."

She found that hard to believe. How in the world had Edward convinced Father to put his name on the guest list?

He answered the question she hadn't asked.

"I told him the truth. I'm in love with you."

* * *

Edward wasn't ready to register the shock on Tirith's face. He hadn't meant to blurt out his feelings quite like that, but nothing about this night had gone right.

"I quit my job." Saying the words still felt a little surreal. In the very best of ways. In the beginning, he hadn't minded when his editor, Holly, had kept him busy, hopping from assignment to assignment. But the CEO wanted higher revenues, Holly had started pushing harder on Edward. This wasn't the first time he'd been encouraged to leave his ethics behind. On other assignment, he'd found ways around compromising his morals. Or hadn't minded so much if digging up a story required getting his metaphorical hands dirty.

Until Tirith.

Knowing Tirith had shined a light on the ugly parts of his job. The parts he couldn't live with any more.

He'd injured his elbow taking Tirith to the ground when the gunshots started. He worried he'd hit her too hard, that maybe she'd been hurt, but she seemed to be unharmed except for the scratch on her face. Maybe that outrageously huge ballgown had some kind of body armor sewn into it.

"You can't quit your job."

It was the last thing he had expected her to say. Maybe *I never wanna see you again* or *leave me alone.*

"The stories you write matter." She blushed, the roses of color striking against her pale skin.

Warmth spread through his chest. Hope surged. "You've read my work?"

Her blush darkened, but she didn't deny it. Her chin jutted out at the stubborn angle he loved so much. "You tell the truth without putting a spin on it. We need more voices like that in the media."

What he really wanted to do was stride over to her and take her in his arms. Reassure himself that she was really all right. Kiss all the fear out of her—out of both of them.

Instead, he went to the door where the security guard had exited and pressed his ear to the portal. He didn't like being trapped in this airless room. Not knowing where the danger was coming from. Not knowing how best to keep Tirith safe. When would the guard be back?

"I can find another job," he said, looking back at her. "My editor and I stopped seeing eye to eye."

He saw the unspoken question in her eyes. He hated to disappoint her, but he wouldn't lie to her again.

"I came here of my own volition. I'm sure your dad has uncovered everything by now. Carrick is my brother. Peyton is my niece."

No surprise crossed her expression, but he saw the hurt. He hated that he was the one who put it there. Even if she never forgave him, she deserved the truth. "You and I met under false pretenses. I engineered our first two meetings. I was trying to get close to you to uncover the facts about the accident. I was sure you'd done something illegal or immoral, and then paid my brother off to make sure it stayed covered up. I was full of self-righteousness. I was wrong. I'm sorry. You'll never know how sorry."

She stood with her hands clasped over her elbows. Holding herself together. "Why haven't you published anything I told you? You're one of the very few people who know about what happened to Maggie and me."

His heart hurt. "Nobody should profit off of what happened to you years ago. That's your story to tell, or keep to yourself."

There was still too much distance between them. Earlier he'd spent fifteen terrifying minutes with her father, confessing his feelings and begging for a chance to apologize and make things right.

He had been gifted these few moments. He wasn't going to waste them by giving up. "I went to see Carrick and Peyton after your father kicked me off the ranch. My brother and I had grown apart, and a lot of that was my fault. We were able to clear the air between us."

Her expression softened.

"We haven't been close for a long time. I tried to take care of him by providing for his physical needs. I hadn't realized... He told me that what he needed from me was... just me." He still got a little choked up over the words. It seemed impossible to believe. He was just Edward. A bit of a workaholic. Nothing to write home about. Not like Tirith and her warm spirit, her kind heart that shined through every action she took. He cleared his throat. "After Carrick set me straight, I realized that maybe what you need from me is the same. Maybe I'm way off base. Maybe you'll never forgive me —and you have a right to feel like that. But I came here tonight to tell you that I love you. I think I started falling for you from the very first time you spoke to me. You surprised me at every turn. I am truly, madly in love with you."

There was a long moment of silence while his heartbeat pounded in his ears. His skin felt hot and prickly, as if he might slip right out of it. Why wasn't she saying anything? Had he gotten it all wrong?

Did she feel nothing for him?

And then he saw that her eyes were welling with tears. She took a step toward him. "Can you come over here?" He'd never heard her speak in such a tremulous, uncertain voice.

"Is that an order, highness?" His heart leaped and he strode toward her. She met him in the middle of the room and came easily into his arms when he reached for her. His own eyes were a little misty as he cupped her cheek in his palm.

"Did you really ask my dad to get you into the ball?"

That was what she wanted to know? "It was terrifying, but I knew that if I wanted to get farther than a few inches in the doorway, I was going to have to win him over."

"I watched footage of you. Of us together."

She had?

"From the day of the chili cook-off. I couldn't stop watching because of how you looked at me."

"I couldn't deny it, even then." He brushed a kiss on her cheek.

"Edward, I fell in love with you too."

His heart beat powerfully in his chest.

"I love you," she whispered.

And he finally let himself do what he had wanted to do since the moment he'd seen her in that crazy dress at the top of the stairs. He bent his head and kissed her.

It was there in the press of her lips against his, the way she touched the back of his neck. He felt how powerfully she loved him. His heart recognized the connection they'd shared from the beginning.

Tirith was a true princess. Goodness radiated from her heart and flowed into everything she did. He didn't deserve her, but he was never going to let her go. He was home now. He'd found what he'd been seeking for so long.

Tirith was it for him.

She broke the kiss, and he realized someone was knocking on the door. He turned their bodies so he was blocking her from whatever danger was coming.

It was Luc, her sister's husband, who stuck his head in the door. "Everyone all right in here?"

"Where's Maggie?" Tirith demanded.

"We're safe," Edward added.

"Maggie's okay. Shaken up."

Tirith relaxed in Edward's arms.

The man went on. "Your mother was injured. I don't know how badly. I can't get any information out of the guards other than that your father took her away."

Edward looked to Tirith, saw the worry and fear in her eyes. He clasped her hand and she clung to him.

Whatever the future held, they would face it together.

Thank you for reading THE TRUE PRINCESS. Read the final book in the Cowboy Fairytales series...

Gideon never stopped loving his princess, though life tore them apart.

When danger threatens, Gideon is the only one who can protect Alessandra.

Isolation means safety, but not for Gideon's heart...

Also by Lacy Williams

Wagon Train Matches series (historical romance)

A Trail So Lonesome

Trail of Secrets

A Trail Untamed

Wind River Hearts series (historical romance)

Marrying Miss Marshal

Counterfeit Cowboy

Cowboy Pride

The Homesteader's Sweetheart

Courted by a Cowboy

Roping the Wrangler

Return of the Cowboy Doctor

The Wrangler's Inconvenient Wife

A Cowboy for Christmas

Her Convenient Cowboy

Her Cowboy Deputy

Catching the Cowgirl

The Cowboy's Honor

Winning the Schoolmarm

The Wrangler's Ready-Made Family

Christmas Homecoming

Heart of Gold

Sutter's Hollow series (contemporary romance)

His Small-Town Girl

Secondhand Cowboy

The Cowgirl Next Door

Cowboy Fairytales series (contemporary fairytale romance)

Once Upon a Cowboy

Cowboy Charming

The Toad Prince

The Beastly Princess

The Lost Princess

Kissing Kelsey

Courting Carrie

Stealing Sarah

Keeping Kayla

Melting Megan

The Other Princess

The Prince's Matchmaker

The True Princess

His Forever Princess

Hometown Sweethearts series (contemporary romance)

Kissed by a Cowboy

Love Letters from Cowboy

Mistletoe Cowboy

The Bull Rider

The Brother

The Prodigal

Cowgirl for Keeps

Jingle Bell Cowgirl

Heart of a Cowgirl

3 Days with a Cowboy

Prodigal Cowgirl

Soldier Under the Mistletoe

The Nanny's Christmas Wish

The Rancher's Unexpected Gift

Someone Old

Someone New

Someone Borrowed

Someone Blue (newsletter subscribers only)

Ten Dates

Next Door Santa

Always a Bridesmaid

Love Lessons

Not in a Series

Wagon Train Sweetheart (historical romance)